The Highland Six Pack's
Cherry

Books in the Highland Six Pack Series:

The Highland Six Pack's Sydney

The Highland Six Pack's Maggie

The Highland Six Pack's Wren

The Highland Six Pack's Cat

The Highland Six Pack's Cherry

The Highland Six Pack's Sadie

The Highland Six Pack's

Cherry

R.S. Oatman

First Edition November 2012

Copyright © 2012 by R.S. Oatman

All Rights Reserved

All of the characters in the Highland Six Pack series are fictitious in that none resemble anyone in particular. They all do, however, represent features and qualities inherent in human nature, and in that regard are portraits in part of each reader. The stories are intended to entertain, be relatable whether obvious or not, and to offer hope of solutions and a hopeful aftermath of traumas common to being alive.

Cover: R.S. Oatman

The cherry blossom: Delicate as it is, this flower has been culturally known to symbolize the intensity of life and the sacrificing of youth to honor superiors.

ISBN-13:978-1481067010

ISBN-10:148106701X

Dedicated to our quest to conquer fear

Preface

Cherry's story is the fifth in the Highland Six Pack series and stands alone, as do the others. Together the books create a bigger package, and this is a good opportunity to share that overview since an insight into simply Cherry is already on the back cover.

The series follow six college roommates as they individually navigate life after graduation in 1971. The times change and the six women change as they grow from their thirties to their sixties and face and conquer the kind of dilemmas and traits we all do in one form or another. We all are part bitchy like Sydney, part reticent like Maggie, and on through the rest as together they make a whole person we recognize as ourselves. Not to entice you to read them all (that's a fib) but you'll see what I mean at the series end.

Here's a brief rundown:

Sydney's early thirties seem to be right on track until life intervenes to show her that keeping a vision isn't easy.

Maggie, in her mid thirties, has to see her mother's influence for what it is and separate parts from herself.

Wren, beautiful Wren, is faced in her early forties with fixing a situation she'd diligently worked to deny.

Cat is still wild and uncontained as she enters her fifties, but tragedy and jolting doubts about her ingrained beliefs are leading her onto a new path.

Cherry's fears, such a part of her, come to a head in her late fifties.

Sadie the dreamer, after a life-changing first love and a marriage to a music star, struggles undeterred to live her own goal at sixty.

Through it all they stay united in a friendship born so long before, and support each other in their relationships, their traumas like abuse, rape, and death, their family issues and careers and their personal concerns of growing older, and through their good times, gloriously good times, all of that binding them in love.

Journey with Cherry and see how and why she is an integral part of the Pack. Prepare your emotions for this one too.

Enjoy!
R.S. Oatman

Chapter 1

For all practical purposes, Cherry had the idyllic life. She and her college sweetheart, married for thirty five years, had raised three lovely children and owned a comfortable home in a small town not far from where she was born. Upstate New York seemed to fit Cherry. She liked its familiarity, she liked its changing seasons, although the summers got too hot and the winter snow left driving too scary. She didn't like her job, was not always fond of her children, questioned her marriage on a daily basis and constantly fought against hope in that regard and most all areas, but otherwise was sufficiently satisfied.

In Cherry's mind, her life was ordinary, the luck of the draw. It was hard to be grateful when so many others had much more. It was hard to face each day knowing nothing exciting would happen, no improvements on existing circumstances, any fun or feeling of peace. That wasn't in the cards for her. It just was the way things were.

That alone, such undeserved mediocrity, would have been difficult enough but, in the recent five years since the terrorist attacks, her doomsday bend took on a sinister reality. Not only had the attacks been too close, they were a sign of further impending danger to all she had ever known. On that eleventh day of September, Cherry, not alone but feeling so, traded her discomfort with life for all-out fear. She kept it hidden the best she could so not to alarm her family. That particular kindness was the way she'd been taught. She didn't know how else to live.

She'd been that way for as long as she could remember. Cherry Rose Gentry, named for both delicate flowers, spent her formative years in the fifties, a product of parents she emulated. Her pink cheeks and angelically soft skin lent themselves to a partial portrayal of such a name but, as her baby stage passed to full childhood, delicate she was not. She was big boned, her mother consoled, and by fifth grade a head taller than even the boys. Though that height spurt would be her last, and she would eventually settle into just a touch above average, the phase left its mark on her already tenuous outlook. Life was not fair. Of that much she was completely, haplessly, certain.

Mr. and Mrs. Gentry hadn't directly intended to stymie their daughter by fostering such an attitude, in fact, they were of the belief they were creating a model Christian citizen. Mrs. Gentry, in particular, saw it as a fulltime and consuming duty to do just that. Children were a gift from God, a gift of such magnitude that any deferring or neglect of righteous instillation was unforgivable. As the family's first such gift, Cherry was not only the opening trial but the recipient of the heaviest dose. The next child was a boy and, maybe for that reason or just his genetic disposition, did not seem to be similarly influenced. Mark freely lived by his own rules. Young Cherry felt it her job to help her mother correct him, strengthening the two females' bond. Their efforts were to no avail, and to make matters worse, Mark seemed to flourish. In all his disruptive disobedience he left Cherry, at a level she couldn't touch, feeling conflictingly envious.

The training of Cherry went beyond the reaches of simply what it took to get into heaven. Her every thought and action became shaped by the subtle, and not so subtle, words spoken and example set by her parents. It wasn't nice to ever act like she was better than anyone else. It was important to know she was. It was always necessary to present a pleasant face even when upset. There was never a valid reason to be upset. She must strive to be the best person she could be. It served no purpose to try to be anything other than what was her calling, one in which she had no say. There was no higher calling than being a wife and mother. That was where her talents lay.

That all may not have left such an indelible mark if not accompanied by additional scruples and Cherry's nature to take everything so meticulously to heart. An early lesson on germs left her washing her hands after any susceptible contact, the threat of their deadly consequences propelling the habit to obsession. Behaviorally, she developed a self punishing need to deny herself treats if she'd erred in even a thought. Her parents deemed her a perfect child, never suspecting her private hell.

One cousin, a girl her age, served as her closest friend, if monthly family visits constituted closeness. Cindy lived one town over and had everything a young girl could want. Her room was decorated in princess pink, her toys and clothes all the best. Cindy had no brother, the ultimate luxury. Cindy found something to giggle about in everything Cherry said and did, a nice giggle, a fun giggle, warming Cherry, until the trips home when her parents' disguised ridicule of wealth made clear as a fog the reason for such giddy happiness. Some people had luck. Some of them didn't deserve luck but they had luck anyway. That was the way the ball bounced. Those people had problems they didn't air. It was good, in the end, that Cindy's family was moving out of state. Cindy wouldn't become a bad influence.

Cherry's teen years came during the tumultuous sixties and war, but local ramifications were isolated and she stayed unaffected. Political dissension and free love would soon be Mark's forte. She behaved, got straight A's, excelled at all she attempted and took on more than her schedule allowed. Those seemed fitting ways to garner her share of attention at home, so otherwise occupied with Mark's antics. On the surface that didn't work, but Cherry knew deep down her parents were proud, prize enough for the moment. She honed a sweet, if often righteously stubborn, disposition to cover her lack of control, a sweetness that would someday lose its fine edge but, for the time being, it became who she was.

Despite her big boned stature's weight, she went out for high school cheerleading, a crowning accomplishment that would come to define her. The school was small, the competition not steep, but the confidence it gave her led to slight rebellions of her parents ways, providing momentary joy yet stronger fear. So ingrained were their values, the slightest variation, a snitched cigarette or beer, left her with disquieting qualms, and she'd quietly retreat after every secret dalliance to the role that gave her parents comfort. It just was the way things were.

She was actually half way popular, and would have been more so if it weren't for the half in her head. Cherry couldn't find who she was. There was her funny side that would erupt for no reason at all, a trait first fostered with love by her cousin, and when she used her softness to its natural peak she could melt hearts and get what she wanted. And then there was her temper, her reaction to anything unseemly, and her unwillingness to accept life at face value. All of this caused her constant debate. Her thoughts would whirl with an underlying torment of possibility taking a wrong direction, only to leave her with no direction at all. At other times, she would act before thinking as if on automatic to avoid any dilemma a thought might present. Those were the times she unintentionally alienated those around her. Try as she might, driven by a universally human need to be loved and accepted, she struggled to see her potential. It was so heartbreakingly not fun being Cherry.

The scruples of her youth had gotten worse before they got better, but by college she'd begun to control them or hide their remaining signs. Combined, though, with her belief in the tenuous operations of life and the randomness of peril, she felt no choice but to cling to them as a shield against all harm. Defending herself from the unknown, whether it was disease or a new idea, was and would be her mode of survival.

Her freshman year away at college changed everything except that, although so much was coming at her so fast she barely could keep a grasp. Nothing felt familiar. The times had brought a campus unrest that was visibly disturbing, chaotic, and even where unseen was still palpable. No one seemed to be behaving the way they'd surely been raised. She had no idea of where she stood on the war or politics in general, but was sure the lurid idea of free expression was leading to moral decay. It'd always been so easy to know the right path. That path no longer existed.

Cherry floundered, concentrating on grades and assignments to ward off the chill. Her dorm roommates quickly stopped asking her to participate or party, and talked, not always discretely, about her rigid standing. Cherry took it with nightly tears. Her only salvation was in knowing she was right, and the fact Thanksgiving would give her the chance to go home.

"They aren't friends, dear, not if they can't accept you the way you are," her mother said, taking the sweet potatoes from Cherry to mash. "You're such a good girl. If they were smart, they'd try to learn a thing or two from you."

"That's pretty hard when they won't even talk to me anymore. They just sit and giggle by themselves. Like hyenas. That's what they sound like. I don't know when they study. Guess they don't. Not my problem if they flunk out. Would serve them right."

"Now Cherry, you know that's not very nice. All you have to be concerned with is your studies. I'm glad you're doing so well. That's what counts." She put down her potholders and searched through a drawer for the yearly used baster. "So, sweetie, have you met any young men in your classes?"

"No." She'd been hoping for an answer to the roommate problem, her most pressing and current dilemma, the one that was ruling her life. Even though finding a husband in college was a preset goal, she so far didn't have the mindset to care.

The best thing about cheerleading, besides its self-esteem building status, had been feeling part of a group of girls. Until then she'd always seemed to have one best friend at a time, one who shared, or allowed, her high standards, and met with her parents' approval. That was alright with Cherry. Home life was so much more comfortable than the strangeness of the outside world. By junior high, with Mark so thoroughly devouring their parents' time and undeniably replacing her as the one in the center, Cherry was pushed to branch out to others. How badly she wanted to fit in somewhere. Her parents rightly encouraged that, hosting sleepovers for whoever would come, but return invitations were few until the glorious years of cheerleading. Her parents chaperoned the bus trips to and from games and held cookouts to celebrate wins. It was a perfect melding of both of her worlds, one she wanted to continue forever.

"You will." Her mother was saying. "There will be someone who sees what a nice person you are. It's just a matter of waiting until he comes along."

Cherry had to test the waters. "What if I don't go back? I mean, I could get a job here, meet somebody that way? Somebody from here would be nicer than the ones from school."

"Uh, you don't know that. There're lots of nice people in the world. I admit, not as many as bad, but all you have to do is study and things will turn around. Daddy and I have faith in you. You'll do fine."

There was no need to bring up quitting again, not this trip, that was quite clear. Throwing a fit or refusing to go was not in the realm of possibility. She let it drop, the question and complaining, and tried to enjoy the brief reprieve of home, all the while dreading the day it would end.

Her mother had been right, as always. The return to school brought a substitute professor, one who didn't appear much older than the students. Mr. Baines had soft, mesmerizing blue eyes and blonde curly hair. He wore a sports coat every day, and took it off as students sat for class. Cherry found this minimal stripping erotic. Surprised at the speed of her quest's end, but accepting it nonetheless, her spirit was renewed. Thank goodness she hadn't dropped out of school. She'd just found her man.

He answered her questions, her rather frequent questions, with the same softness his eyes exuded. She started coming to class as early as her previous one allowed, hoping to catch him alone, but since he habitually appeared just in the nick of time, she changed her strategy to lingering after class. That didn't work either. He was a hard man to corner.

She kept her newfound exhilaration about college to herself, having no one who cared to know, and began to take extra effort in her appearance. One roommate noticed, and offered to lend Cherry a green sweater that matched her green plaid slacks. That tidbit of friendship opened the door to a better evening that day, then the next, with Cherry never seeing the original problem as her own imagination and disposition the whole time. Full inclusion never came, but at least dorm life was now tolerable.

It was nearly Christmas before she summoned the nerve to approach Mr. Baines between classes. By then the one-sided romance had grown in Cherry's mind to a full, two-way hot love. His eyes, as he'd stroll the aisles through seated students and stop to answer her questions, said he got it. He knew how she felt and he felt the same. One of them had to make a move. He likely was waiting for it to be her.

The door to his classroom was closed. Opening it was going to take more courage than Cherry had assumed would be needed. Her hand reached for the knob, then stopped. He may be busy and upset at an interruption. It was important to catch him in a good mood. But if he was busy he could just say so and no harm would be done. The closed door was actually good. She could shut it behind her since that was how he seemed to like it. Perfect. This was a private type meeting.

Maybe he wasn't even in there. The only way to find out was to try. She reached for the knob again and this time turned it quietly but confidently. Life was about giving new things a chance, wasn't that what she was trying to learn? Her heart pounded, her carefully prepared words raced in random order. The door opened, and as she was about to take her first step in, her eyes traveled from the knob to Mr. Baines desk. He was standing in front of it, lip locked in a heavy kiss, so heavy he didn't look up, with someone else. A brunette. That's all she could see or absorb. Cherry couldn't help but stare as the color of her dreams washed from her face. If he'd only look up and see what he'd done to her, that would have been some consolation. But he didn't. She backed away into the emptiness of a world without him in it.

"Hey, wait up!"

For the briefest of seconds her mind played out a full fantasy. It was him, rushing to tell her it'd been a mistake. He was so sorry she'd seen that. It hadn't meant anything. He loved just her, with his whole heart.

"You dropped this."

She turned to take her notebook from the outstretched hand of a boy.

"Sorry to yell," he said, ignorantly walking along side her. "Just wanted to make sure I'd catch you. See you've got Romeo too. Turning in your project? I've got him seventh hour. Ours aren't due until break."

She wouldn't have heard him anyway, but the words after Romeo blurred as if one. She'd been such a fool. There was nothing worse than being a fool. Mr. Baines was apparently someone everyone wanted. He had his pick. It wasn't her. Not even close. She hadn't stood a chance. How stupid to think he'd want her.

"I'm Jeff," the voice said, still tagging beside her. "Conlon."

"Hi. And thanks. I've gotta go." She veered to the right at the first exit.

"Maybe I'll see you around."

She didn't answer. She hadn't even really seen his face. But a few days later in the cafeteria, as he stood over her, tray in hand, asking to join her for lunch, a vague familiarity returned. With the faintest of smile, Cherry nodded okay.

She was in no mood to visit, let alone to find anyone attractive who wasn't Mr. Baines. It hadn't been easy getting over him. There was no one to talk to about it, no one who could have been trusted with such an embarrassing secret. She'd put on a brave face with her roommates and, after regaining her composure, continued to function as if nothing had happened. She'd even dared to look Mr. Baines in the eye during the first class after catching him, hoping to feel a diminished love since he was obviously such a jerk, but it had hurt. At least this semester was close to an end.

"So, again, I'm Jeff. Nice to meet you, uh…?"

"Cherry. Sorry."

"That's a fine name. No need to be sorry."

His smile was catchy. She smiled back at him. It then became a fairly pleasant half hour of talk, most of it giving her a much needed lift. Jeff was having a hard time too, feeling a part of this campus. She didn't admit to that, of course, but instead offered a few tips on how to ignore all the bad. Having that tidbit of regained control gave Cherry a sense of accomplishment, and by the time Jeff had to head off for class, Cherry felt like she'd found her first compatible friend.

She didn't suspect he'd pegged her insecurities and had vented imaginary ones to connect. He hadn't really lied, he had common freshman quandaries too, but had quickly seen those as the best way to reach her so he stayed with them and embellished ever so slightly. He liked her. He wasn't sure why, but he did. It wasn't easy meeting girls, not girls who'd seem likely to want him. Cherry had a sweet vulnerability about her that said she was in need of someone to help her through this new maze. She would also, hopefully, be open to liking him for more than just that.

For the next few weeks until their semester break, Jeff seemed to find her wherever she went. It always appeared coincidental until it happened just too many times. Cherry, with each passing day lessening the pain and humiliation of her professor crush, thought it flattering and gave into Jeff's presence, not the least of her reasons being the fact she could go home at Christmas and announce a new boyfriend. He was okay in a scrawny sort of way, his smile was nice and he had good teeth and eyes that twinkled at her when staring. He was kind of tall, or looked that way because of his skinny frame, with fairly wide shoulders - a plus, and a butt that would have looked invitingly tight if it weren't sizes smaller than hers. He didn't swear and he made her feel wanted. That was enough for now.

Their happenstance meetings led to evening trips after Christmas down the street to Jimmy's Place, the local college hangout, and a kiss at her dorm door when he dropped her off following the second one. It was her first real tongue in throat kiss, thrust by a drunk and impatient Jeff, seizing the opportunity and testing his luck. Cherry, having had a few too many beers herself, responded with unfamiliar but toe tingling zeal. Her mother's enthusiasm at Christmas over this new found love had seemed to give unspoken permission to go with this flow. Anything that felt this supernaturally high had to be alright in what was becoming an adult life. It was also a good way to keep him. She waited until his hands slid from her back to just under her arms before she pulled away for the night. He knew she knew he'd just copped a feel of the sides of her breasts, and she acknowledged it with a look that said it was fine. That would bring him back for more, but the rest had to be planned and special.

It would be premarital sex, of course, something the younger Cherry had vowed against. That had been a naïve girl's dream. This was the real world. Survival in this world meant bending but not breaking her values, never losing sight of the spirit of the rules. Somehow she had to fit. It looked so easy for others. No one could possibly understand how hard this was for her, but it didn't matter anymore. Nothing mattered but making it work.

She invited him up to her room on a night the others were partying. The implication was clear, and Jeff was as nervous as she was. He'd had only the briefest experience once before, brief due to his over excitement, a worry that came with him that night. His mind was soon put to rest. Cherry, dressed in a frilly front button blouse, the top three left undone, opened the door with the weakest of smiles, her eyes betraying her fears. After a few awkward moments of conversation, he just held her, whispering reassurance into her ear and asking over and over if she was sure. She was, in words. His protective nature waylaid his own anxiety and he took over as if more seasoned than he felt. It was earth moving for neither, although satisfying for Jeff, but the shared intimacy of it was important to both. That kind of caring was mutually their nature, unlike others both knew who so carelessly gave without love. It seemed, from that encounter forward, they had found in each other a soul mate.

The year had been one of transitioning, and Cherry, in all of her complexities, had landed with a familiar footing. She'd managed to find what she'd come to find, without giving up too much of herself. Jeff wasn't Mr. Baines but he was comfortable. The Mr. Baineses of the world were for other people, lucky people. It made sense in her seasoned logic, and that alone made it somehow alright. Her roommates and the campus had fallen into place too, now that she'd concretely faced to truth of haves and have-nots. She'd painfully learned to accept and adapt, adjusting her stance and beliefs and outlook to her surroundings while never letting go of their core. It was who she was. It was simply the way things were.

It seemed the final step to full maturity. Unfortunately, it pretty much was.

Chapter 2

The girls in the Highland Street rental were nice, ordinary girls, not homecoming queens or anything like that, all except for Wren who, as luck would have it, was her roommate in the three bedroom house. Wren was everything Cherry was not, at least in Cherry's mind. Wren was an outward picture of utter perfection with an enchanting personality to match. And an actual high school homecoming queen. Nothing about her said she had any inner demons. Wren was another example of life's unfairness, not Wren's fault and Wren was hard to dislike anyway, but the irony didn't escape Cherry. Life was going to make sure she fully grasped the fact not all its children were equal.

The move sophomore year from the dorms to this rental house had been her parent's idea. Cost and availability left other arrangements out of the question. If she'd learned nothing else about living with girls, it was how to blend without bending, so she accepted the move as just another test of her will. Nothing about it at that point would tell her this was to be a life changing event.

At least these girls were more open to her than the dorm ones had been until turning fairly decent toward the end. From the first day, these five seemed to actually like her. They all were so different and had nothing in common except the fact they were here to make it through school, especially Sydney, so tall and standoffish, who simply did her thing with no bother to make any kind of impression. She was nice, though, in a bit of a patronizing way but that was completely tolerable.

To find her place and a way to fit, Cherry set out to claim a spot as the one to keep the place clean. She'd done her share of housework at home so was no stranger to how it should be done, and she liked the feeling it gave of purpose and accomplishment. Also was the fact she operated best when all things were in their rightful state. Sydney often helped, just to get it done. Sydney maybe had the same need for order. Just do it, she always said. That apparently applied to all things in her life. Sydney was an unstoppable machine. How nice it would be to have some of that, but it was a trait a person had or didn't. Lucky Sydney.

Cherry found herself looking up to Sydney, and would have loved a close friendship with her, but Sydney had that with Maggie, the two tied since childhood. Maggie was so quietly friendly there was no way to resent her for having the coveted side by side spot. Those two shared something special, understandably, so to horn in wouldn't have done any good. Sadie, a teenage looking girl with long curly hair and a habit of singing at odd times, would have made for a best friend if she hadn't had such a free spirited personality. She just didn't think the same way about things. That was fine, Sadie didn't impose on anyone else's way, but she wouldn't have made for a close friend. As a roommate, though, Sadie was pleasantly acceptable.

That would have all been fine, but then there was Cat. The Lord only knew why she'd been pitted with Cat. Cat was like Mark, never minding anything conventional or sensible. Cat was disruptive, crude, had no modesty or clue of proper behavior. Cat did and said whatever she wanted and, soon to become apparent, got a weird kick out of picking on her. Cherry was initially taken aback, not used to special attention of any kind, but before too long into the living situation she found a retaliating voice. She'd done so with Mark; she could do so with Cat. Cat had to be put in place.

The strange thing was, Cat seemed to like the reprimands. She didn't obey, that was immediately evident, but she responded to Cherry's corrections with a noticeable flair. They soon became the center of the household's energy, Cat doing that quite well on her own but bringing Cherry into the mix added spice.

With the exception of Cat, and even because of Cat, Cherry had found a place of acceptance. However, Cherry being Cherry, with her esteem in constant jeopardy, she wasn't comfortable in this comfort. Against a nag of a new better judgment, she retreated to coping the only way she knew how. She found fault. Sydney was too confident with no grounds for being so. Someday she'd get her comeuppances. Maggie often was overly nice, leaving others to question her true opinion. Wren, well, Wren had to have something wrong that just wasn't visible. No one, not even the luckiest person, is really that totally perfect. And Cat. Enough said.

Apparently, though, these roommates were too preoccupied to notice the shift in her thoughts. They continued to treat her as though she was one of them. She hid well her innermost ideas of their worth until, just months into the harboring of those secret animosities, she relented to giving them up. The girls weren't so bad. Sydney talked to her almost like an equal sometimes while they cleaned together. Maggie gave her a gorgeous cardigan after just one compliment on it. Wren was starting to seem more like a real person after sharing bedtime stories about boys. They really were quite good people. Even, with reservations, Cat.

It would be years and years before Cherry would learn they all had had coping ways of their own. These girls were as confused as she was about who they were behind how they were raised, each so differently yet much the same, and how to apply that to who they were to become. With every day bringing the future their way at a speed that blurred their minds, coupled with the change of the times, it was no wonder they, in part like every generation before them, felt simultaneously the weight and lightness and responsibility of life on their undeveloped shoulders. That much they voiced at the time in roundabout ways that skirted any hint of a grasp.

Sydney was working overtime on her confident stride to cover her own unnamed anxieties. Maggie was pinning her entire future on the love she had for Sydney's brother, a relationship that to others seemed doomed. Wren, in all of her perfection, felt nothing like the exterior she presented. Her life, too, hinged on acceptance by men. Sadie, so exuberant about love and life, was bracing against unforeseen disappointment. In that regard, she and Cheery seemed alike. The difference was Sadie kept hope.

Cat was the only one immune that year, only because Cat's pace left no time for worry. She was involved in the time's politics, hell bent on saving the world, and busied herself in every spare moment with a connected or not entertainment. Cat's kind of fun made Cherry cringe, the others agreed to a point. They delicately suggested Cat's free love not be public, but drew a firmer line at her in-house pot use, not having Cherry's disgust but wanting to avoid group arrest. Cherry, the instigator of straightening that particular offense, felt little satisfaction when Cat cheerfully admitted she should have thought of it first. A semblance of contrition for using at all would have been much more appropriate. Heaven only knew what else she was taking that could lead to horrible consequences. It surprised Cherry to feel that Cat's well being mattered.

Although she could never completely drop her private resentments, her depths always needing a shield, the lessening of them as the months wore on gave Cherry, for the first time since college and even before, a security she so longed to have. And when the time came to re-up for the next year, and she was asked to please say yes, Cherry, of course, did. By then they were known as the Highland Six Pack by the gang at Jimmy's. It'd be a shame to break up the Pack. It'd be a worse shame to be left out in the cold and face two more years of college alone.

There was still Jeff, a regular now at the Highland house and a friend to the girls as well. He and Cherry seemed joined at the hip, or did until Cat made the suggestion she not settle. It began and ended, as did all of the exchanges between them, in Cherry's denial of any worth in what Cat said. Why she even listened, she didn't know.

"I'm just saying, Cherry Blossom," Cat said, not suspecting the truth of that name. "He's your first. Your first lay, anyway. You have sacked him, right?"

"That's none of your business, Cat. But yes. We've done it."

"Well, good. But what I'm saying is, how do you know what else is out there? I mean, I like Jeff, he's great. But he doesn't seem to push you, to challenge you. He's like an old shoe. You're used to each other, but that seems all you two have going."

"So what's wrong with that? Not everybody likes being pushed or whatever."

"Doesn't mean it's not good for a person."

"What, I'm supposed to go out whoring every night? You think I have to try on every guy to know for sure? I'm not you. That's not who I am."

"Seeing as how I know you're not trying to hurt my feelings, I'll put it another way. Loosen up, for God's sake. Just explore. It certainly can't hurt. If Jeff's the one, he'll be there when you're done. That's all I'm saying. Live a little. Take some chances."

"You sound like my brother. That's how he operates. And look where it's gotten him. I'm sure he's out at this very moment fighting against the war, just like you, but he doesn't have a job, has no idea what he wants to do with his life. Girl friends up the whazoo, though, so what the heck. That'd be his take on it."

"Sounds like somebody I'd like to meet."

Cherry rolled her eyes. Cat could push all she wanted, but it wasn't going to do any good. The Cats and Marks of the world were the reason there was such chaos lately. Somebody had to use common sense. Somebody had to keep values alive. She shouldn't be made to feel like she was the one in the wrong. How stupid was that.

Skinny Cat, who never had to worry about weight, or mascara to make her lashes show up, and never burned in the sun but always looked tan, was so unfairly secure. That's probably where she got her whole personality. No concerns ever about how she looked made her free to be so outrageous. Yes, it'd be nice in a way to be like that, with no fear ever of retribution, but it wasn't right. It was good of Cat to take the time to try to help her, and was a sign of strength that Cat, although way off base, felt as strongly as she did about her own ways. Overbearing and opinionated as the talks could get, it was nice having Cat care like she did.

That alone gave her reason to think.

Cat's words naturally aside, Cherry broke up with Jeff a few weeks later, only to find nothing else out there. Not that there weren't any nice guys in some of her classes, the issue was getting to know them. Lonesome and uneasy in this new kind of setting, she promptly took back Jeff, a pattern that would repeat itself throughout most of the year. She liked Jeff, she did, but he had become a bit boring. Being with him was often like having the type of brother she always thought Mark could be if he tried. In that much, at least, she found a satisfying need fulfilled.

That third year in the Highland house, the last before graduation, saw Cherry stretch as much as she could. She'd found her place amongst the girls and was flourishing in her special role. They weren't really a family, and the bond surely wouldn't last, but she'd found in them what she'd hoped. A place to fit. She had grown to admire the person she was and had no desire to change. Change wasn't necessary when everything worked, if not perfectly, perfection not to be expected. It just was the way things were.

During the winter of their last year, as the time approached for the Highland Six Pack to disband, they instead seemed to merely grow closer. Cherry now made a point to join them on every Friday and Saturday night outings to Jimmy's, leaving Jeff behind if and when they were a couple, knowing he'd be there if and when she wanted him. Being part of this circle had always felt good and this was their last year as roommates. She drank right along with them, often too much, but passed on anything more than just beer. A good girl had her limits.

There was a bunch of guys, regulars, who had befriended them all as a group. They weren't the dating kind, Cat had a corner on that, if that could be called dating, but simply added spice to the round table fun. They also partnered well for dancing when the beer kicked in enough to render them embarrass proof. They were just guys, friends, an extension of the Highland Six on those nights. Most were cute, though a bit wild and not marriage material, but Cherry enjoyed their attention immensely.

Nick, a soft spoken, great looking one, their unofficial leader, was tempting regardless, although she was certain he was way out of her league. He was a tall, burly guy with arms that looked like they could lift up the bar. His charm extended to everyone, including her, while the others seemed to focus on boisterous Cat. And Wren, of course, when Wren wasn't off with her boyfriend. Nick was different. Nick was worth bending some rules.

His talk of childhood made him sound to be from her same background, a hard working middle class family. He was carrying a part time job to work his way through college, something she didn't have to do but she admired those who did. He'd given up sports just to carry the load but never complained about having to do so. It seemed, though, by this senior year, the load was taking a toll.

"Looks like Flannigan's not going to cut me any slack," he said to whoever was listening. "Leaves me two credits short of graduating. Anybody ever have Worski? Have to take him to make it up. Hope he's easy."

"He's an asshole, Nick," Cat said, trying to hide a smirk at his unintended innuendo.

"He is not," chided Sydney. "He's fine. At least that's what I've heard."

"Yeah, he is. I just had him." Cherry, as was par, spoke without understanding it'd get her uninvited laughs.

"Come on, you guys. You all know I mean. I just had his class. He's fair. He's okay."

"Good. That's what I was hoping. So, kiddo, got any old tests or stuff?"

Cherry was in a spot. Cheating wasn't like upstanding Nick, he must be desperate, but it also wasn't in her to do. This was Nick, though. It still was cheating. He gratefully came to her rescue.

"That was stupid. Sorry. It's just that I have to pass. I have to."

Cherry wasn't ready to pass up this opportunity, or have the occasion end with her coming off as a prude. "I would if I could but I didn't keep any. But I can still help you with it, if you want me to."

"Really? Thanks, kid. You bet."

So began Cherry's late nights of tutoring Nick at his apartment. Innocent and needed as the tutoring was for Nick, Cherry enjoyed the sessions far beyond the studies. The one on one connection, with Nick's face along side hers deep in a book, the light conversation between the pages, was the fulfillment of a dream image she'd kept buried since puberty. Nick was so handsome, so rugged, so popular, so interested in all she had to say, whether pertaining to the work or not. He was fast becoming her friend. A special friend. Maybe never a boyfriend, but this was second best.

Once comfortably into their sessions, Cherry rewarded his studious efforts one night by bringing a six pack of beer. Studying doesn't have to be dull or all work, she announced. He agreed. The next time she did again. The beer gave her courage to be just a tad friendlier than normal and eventually totally his, if just for a moment in time.

"Nick," she said, one night taking his face and turning it to her. "Kiss me."

Nick obliged with a plant of a soft kiss on her lips. Cherry held him, opening her mouth for more. He again rose to the moment. She slid her hand between their close bodies to unbutton her blouse, but at that signal for more, Nick took over for her. He gently caressed her clothed breast in a circular motion, leaving her nipple ignored. That would come after the anticipation had built. When the arch of her body said the feeling had sufficiently peaked, he went under her bra for the touch.

Cherry, her crotch suddenly on fire, reached for his.

"Well, aren't you the little tiger," he said into her ear as he eased her flat with the couch. "Are you sure about this?"

She could only nod and shut her eyes, signs of further permission. Cherry was, willingly and with few hesitations, already transported to another reality.

In all of her times having sex with Jeff, she'd never had it like this. Nick took charge, loving her with careful yet reckless abandon, a mix that allowed her to fully release. He moaned and he grunted, so thoroughly enjoying himself. Cherry did the same in return. It was fun and freeing and, for the first time in her life, she climaxed. Twice. Jeff always tried by working really hard but never could get it just right. With Nick it just happened, the first one rolling throughout her body as his hand found and stayed on the spot. The second came with him in her, a surprise one that just exploded and was heightened by the match of their yells.

Cherry's spent body walked itself home that night, thoughts of the encounter whirling in a euphoric spin. She'd slept with Nick. He'd slept with her. What an unbelievable experience. This was the beginning of her life finally unfolding. She'd done it. She'd asked and she'd gotten her share of luck. She'd had incredible sex with Nick. From the first kiss and the smell of his breath to his tender afterwards peck on her lips, it'd been the most incredible experience in life so far.

That feeling lasted just until she got into her pajamas and bed. Surfacing details were reminding her of all the noises she'd made, and she felt a discomforting embarrassment. He must not think her very lady-like. The next occasion she'd be quieter, she'd show him she could be as feminine as any other girl he'd had. She replayed the entire event over and over, each time minimizing her unwanted parts. It had been so terrific otherwise, so unbelievably, magically terrific. It would have been better if he'd done the initiating, though, that would have made it perfect, except for her noises, but he hadn't. Any pride she had in being the instigator seemed now inappropriately placed. He should have been the one. Next time she'd let him take the lead. How stupid to let these little things ruin what was such an earthmoving night. And yet they persisted into the dawn.

There was to be no next time with Nick.

"You know what, kiddo," he said at their next session as she inched a bit closer to his side. "I'm thinking we need to cool it. It just isn't the best idea. Don't get me wrong, I enjoyed every minute of it, but you've got a boyfriend who probably wouldn't be real nuts about it if he knew…"

"No I don't. We're not seeing each other anymore."

Well, be that as it may, I guess I just have to say nope, we better not." He reached over for a brotherly pat to her head. "Hate to take a chance at messing up our neat friendship, you know? So, let's get crackin' here, teacher." With that he winked and opened a book.

Cherry felt her heart drop to the floor. She hadn't had any long range plans to marry him, although that certainly would have been the ultimate outcome, but she was deeply hurt by the horrendous feeling of rejection and the denial of a chance to show him her best. Nick was to have been a move up in life, a way to show the others who she really was inside of the shell they assumed. He was to prove luck could happen to her. In the flash of that instant he'd rendered her back to her stance. She wasn't one luck opted to choose.

The lessons continued under the buddy guise, a role better than not feeling special at all. In between they still met with the bunch at Jimmy's, both pretending like nothing had happened. Cherry's spirit, so flimsily hanging on by a thread, had been trampled to dust the Friday night, a week after her sex with Nick, when he left with a girl he'd apparently just met that evening. Visions of the passion she'd shared with him flashed through her mind and felt ugly. Nick, handsome and cool not withstanding, was a pig. She had been such a fool. If she worked at it, she could forget.

That may have been possible if by March, her period had come on time. She was never, ever, late. The first week without it dragged day by day, with checks in a bathroom after each class, the fear mounting as no sign appeared. This just couldn't be. She hadn't been with Jeff since right after Christmas, and had had a period since then. He'd always pulled out in time anyway. Why hadn't she made Nick do the same? How could one night with him end up like this? It wasn't fair. And then she remembered. Life wasn't.

By the third week she knew she had to do something. There was a chance this could not be the end of the world. She rehearsed the words she'd say to Nick. He wouldn't have to marry her; she'd make that gesture clear, leaving room for him to step up to the plate and offer the honorable solution himself. A baby is a happy thing. Being a father is one of life's joys. She'd be sorry it had happened without any plan, but now wasn't the time for regret. He was going to be a father. They maybe could call him Nick Junior.

"Hey Cher, get the message from Nick?" Sadie asked as Cherry passed through the kitchen. "Said he doesn't need you tonight. Guess the test this week was canceled or something."

"Oh. No, I didn't get it, so thanks."

"Want to do something? I'm going to Jimmy's, but not till later. We could hang out at the Center until then."

"Thanks," Cherry said, fighting to get words through the lump in her throat. "Think I'll just go to the library. Need to get caught up with my own stuff. He's been taking a lot of time."

"Yeah, I gather that. Sounds like you're doing a good job, though. Can't be easy, I bet really understanding the stuff isn't at the top of his list."

Cherry managed a chuckle to cover her nerves. "That's an understatement! It's okay, I haven't minded. See you later, okay?"

After beating a hasty exit, Cherry wasn't sure where to go. The library would be the honest place, since that's where she'd told Sadie she'd go, and a way to be left alone. Although, who cared. Little white lies had been coming easier each year as she'd been forced to meld into life. Making up an excuse just to save face wasn't a big deal, no one was harmed. Her pace slowed as she neared then passed the library. There. She'd gone to the library, she just hadn't gone in, so she hadn't really lied. And so what if she had. She settled on dismissing it as inconsequential.

Before too long, she would become very good at doing that in a much, much bigger way.

Tonight had to be the night. If she waited, she might lose her nerve. She turned the corner and headed to Nick's apartment. He'd be home yet, this wasn't a work night for him and partying didn't start until dark. The sight of his building made her heart race. This was it. This night would change her life.

She climbed the dark stairwell to his third floor apartment. The stairwell had always given her such exciting anticipation and a feeling of being one of the top popular girls. She'd be going to Nick's at his request. Her. Cherry Gentry. She'd always felt honored, even after his hurtful rebuttal. The thrill seemed silly in a way, yet not enough to think otherwise.

This time was different. There was no thrill involved. He didn't know she was coming, nor would he be prepared for her news. He may not take this calmly. There was that possibility. She'd have to word it carefully, lead him into it so it wasn't a shock. The words jumbled in her brain. Maybe she should just blurt it. This was his fault as much as hers, if not more so. She shouldn't have to be this afraid. He's the one who should worry about how to take care of her, make sure she wasn't upset. She was carrying his baby, after all.

The music coming from his room floated down the hall at the landing. Cherry walked to his door and knocked. No answer. He probably couldn't hear with the music so loud. She tried the knob. The door opened. She called his name without answer. He obviously was here, that much was apparent, so she entered a few steps and called again. The place was in the usual disarray, empty pizza boxes and beer bottles on the table, two full ashtrays and a half eaten sandwich on the counter. She called once more as she made her way to the living room. That was as far as she went.

There was his bare butt in the air, pumping someone beneath him. Just as the girl's legs rose to wrap around him in peaking intensity, Cherry turned to make her way to the hall, not feeling the impact until she reached the stairwell. With the familiar handrail guiding her, the sentiment of it not helping, wrenching tears washed away any remaining rainbow. It was over. She'd known he was a player, but seeing it was different. It had never mattered exactly like this. He wasn't father material. Or husband. She was very much alone with just a baby. He was out of the picture.

She needed a few days stall to call Jeff, who came immediately at her beckoning. Yes, of course, he'd reconcile, he'd missed her so much he'd gone crazy. And then she spilled her news. She couldn't tell him the real truth, that would hurt his feelings, so she concocted an angle that didn't place blame on her or – in the name of forgiveness and God's plan – the contributing party, and through more tears added it was too painful to talk about regardless so please would he understand and not push.

Jeff was completely sympathetic and held her, assuring her he'd take good charge. They could get married as soon after graduation as possible. He'd get a teaching job wherever she wanted to live, and she could stay home with the baby. They would forget this had happened and raise the child as theirs. This would all be alright. It really would. They never have to tell anyone the baby wasn't his.

The arrangements made announcing the situation to the girls much easier. Getting pregnant was just something that happened when people fooled around like they had. No one thought to count any sequence of dates, something that had anyway grown hard to keep track. They were happy for her and passed no judgment. At least none Cherry could know. Their secret concern had nothing to do with the surprise pregnancy; it was her love for Jeff they questioned. At this point, however, that was not theirs to voice, so they kept mum about any misgivings. This was dear Cherry's life. They wished her, with all their hearts, a future of joy and happiness.

Cherry intended to give it a shot.

Chapter 3

Cherry loved her baby like she had never loved anyone else in her life. Most of the time. At others, with just a glance, she'd see Nick or remember the night, and then that love took on a strange hue. Her mind could not get passed it. On the one hand, that night had been the absolute pinnacle of her life, on the other, the eve of destruction. Combined, it had rendered this child, an innocent by-product of the workings of life, first and foremost as proof of the rule of unfairness. Cherry was sure her gradual venturing outside of her zone to prove the rule wrong had culminated in the fate of that night. Never again would she listen to anything but what was buried deep within her. Others could maybe work around theirs, but she no longer would try.

Jenny had Nick's light wavy hair, the color able to pass for hers but not its fineness and curls. Above that, she had Nick's personality. She was a wild child from the day she was born, Nick and Cat and Mark all rolled into one. She seemed to never need sleep, and bulked at Cherry's set structure of feeding. As a toddler, she was into everything not put outside of her reach, her curiosity and disobedience growing with each passing day. It was the beginning of a life of being regularly grounded and sent to her room to ponder her misbehavior. Cherry, unable to let her grow up like Mark, made shaping Jenny a primary duty. That was the least she could do to salvage this child she'd so unwontedly brought into the world.

One by one, the two baby boys to follow each had Jeff's darker hair, skinny build, and calm dispositions. Everyone remarked what a cute family they were, the boys so much like their father and the girl a blonde like her mother. The talk served to help cover the lie and should have made Cherry feel better, but instead became a constant reminder of the falsehood of her life.

Jenny was kind to her brothers, although mixed it with a penchant for teasing them. Cherry saw the kindness as the one redeeming quality her daughter had. The teasing, however, was a source of never ending reprimands, since it led to the boys getting even and disrupting the household on an hourly basis. Curbing Jenny, though a fruitless endeavor, was the only way to maintain a semblance of peace. Cherry's need to alter such unruly behavior and her resentment of Jenny's heritage became indistinguishably intertwined.

By then they had moved from a small apartment to a larger one to finally a house, as Jeff's teacher's pay allowed, each within miles of her parents. That was a blessing beyond anything else Cherry knew. Past the solace of familiar surroundings was the ongoing help from her mother, help that came through baby sitting, cleaning, guidance and forthright direction. As couples, they picnicked together, took family trips to the zoo, with Jeff and her father getting along as well as she did with her mother. They were Cherry and Jeff's best and only real friends.

As Jenny grew, she would have turned to those grandparents if she could have, but that just wasn't the case, given they were carbon copies of her own parents. At thirteen she ran away, only to be brought back by squad car. What she was running from, she didn't know. It just felt like basic survival.

Jenny didn't seem to have Cat or Mark's good natured sense of adventure and lark within her rebellion. Hers was different, more defiant in a meaningless way. At least it appeared that way to Cherry. Not having ever experienced any real need to rebel, dealing with Jenny was outside of a relating realm. None of her efforts ever soaked into Jenny, in fact, Jenny delighted in riling her mother to the point of sometimes near blows. Spanking had never been Cherry's method, but as Jenny grew in size and attitude, the temptation to strike her occurred more than once. Cherry resisted but was at a loss for a replacement way to get through to her and have Jenny follow her lead. Because of Jenny, the household, including at times the marriage, was in rather constant turmoil. For Cherry, this was a foreign, yet in many ways familiar, way to live.

Jeff didn't have it in his makeup to ever throw in Cherry's face Jenny's unorthodox origin. And he loved Jenny as he did the boys. She loved him in return, very much, but was highly disappointed his word didn't hold water when it came to child rearing decisions. Jeff understood her frustration and had some himself but, in the name of upholding the peace, he simply carried out Cherry's wishes. Jenny's attempts to have him take a stand were met with reminders that a family runs best when all get along. Over the years, Jenny quit asking. Her dad, his love aside, was no help at all.

The relationship Jenny had with Cherry had love on both sides too. Jenny would have liked nothing better than to have her mother love her, like her, approve of her, or even just accept her the way she was. On that front, Jenny would never stop trying, despite outward appearances. It was the motivation behind all she did, even the running away. She had hoped with everything in her that her mother would see that and be so distraught that a happier home life would follow. Cherry's reaction was instead one of complete disgust and distrust. She grounded Jenny from all school activities, restricted her to her room after school, and turned a cool ear to Jenny's begs for forgiveness. A child must be taught in no uncertain terms just what behavior was tolerated.

So Jenny tried again, plotting and scheming her way at fourteen to run to a neighboring town, far enough so finding her would take more than just a few days. Maybe then her mother would have time to realize how much she should treasure her. That time instead got her a two week lockup in juvie, Cherry not visiting once.

There was no way, in Cherry's set mind, that to go there and chance inadvertently exposing her true emotions would amount to anything worthwhile. She bottled all of her worry, heartache, and fears and stayed away in hopes Jenny would see that such antics had just made things much worse. Any admittance of weakness, as she saw it, was setting a bad example. She was the mother. Respect for a mother was the way to learn how to be a functioning adult. Being soft, being a friend or an understanding cohort wasn't going to produce good results. Cherry believed that completely, as much as it hurt to not race for a forever tight hold of her precious little girl the night Jenny was found unharmed.

Her pain was as deep as her belief she was right. Caught between what she wanted and what she saw fit to do, Cherry was a frazzled mess. How badly she wished she could accept Jenny as she was, her free spirit and all, a spirit that actually had more than a little appeal. To be that free of guilt and rules and conscience was asking for far too much, but there had to be a way to be free within certain frames. If only she could learn that from Jenny and not give up her sense of self. Those moments of weakness, and that was how Cherry viewed them, came often enough to be disturbing. She couldn't give in to them. She had to be the mother. The best mother she could be.

It didn't help that her own mother, with similar good intentions, was always on hand with advice and to remind Cherry of the necessity to squelch all unacceptable behavior. Jenny needed the kind of guidance that could only come from an unwavering position of authority. In her gentlest voice, her words yet sharp as cut glass, she made it clear Cherry was slacking somehow. Never mind that such tactics had failed with her Mark. This was a chance for reprieve.

What she didn't know was the extra and secret burden Cherry was carrying about the circumstance of Jenny's conception. There were times the remembrance even for Cherry faded out of sight when discipline measures momentarily overruled. Then the thought would return. Her digression from all she knew to be good made this her fault and had caused this kind of punishment. It certainly wasn't Jenny's fault, poor Jenny had nothing to do with how she was born. Cat would say every immaterialized soul has the choice of when and where it comes, but that was hooey. Cherry tried to take the penance that was Jenny with a swallowed pride. This outcome was just the way things were.

The boys, Steve and Bruce, named after their grandfathers, had eventually begun to play off of the family discontent in addition to fighting with their sister. Cherry loved them as she did Jenny, and raised them with the same array of principles, rules that Steve actually somewhat embraced but younger Bruce rarely saw as needed or fun. Acting like Jenny got a bigger response. He didn't, however, have Jenny's edge. His was contained to just mischief. That Cherry could handle.

Amidst the chaos of those young family days, Cherry lost track of herself. She kept the habits of her youth, never stopping to question their worth, her unchecked fears mounting with each passing year. Middle age was upon her before it seemed time, her youth and all of its promise not to be hers again. It helped to know that the Highland girls, each in their individualized way, were experiencing the same kind of loss, though they didn't seem to mind as much, or have such a sense of finality. They still had dreams and plans and projects and were excited about what lay ahead in their lives. For Cherry, living was merely a matter of having more of the same.

That could have been a blessing, if it had happened that way. At eighteen, Jenny left home, never to return as their child. The note said she was pregnant and going to start a new life with boyfriend Kyle. This time was different. This time it wasn't a cry for help or a way to get her parents attention. Jenny had quit, she was done trying. There was no use in tracking her down, the note said, she wouldn't come back if found. No one could make her. That was the law.

Jeff was beside himself, and used every waking moment to question where she might be and how to fix this. He talked to Kyle's parents who had no idea, then rounded up Jenny's friends for clues. The friends, shrugging their shoulders, knew, he could just tell. So did Kyle's parents who, during a second visit, admitted as much. As parents themselves, they sympathized, but Jenny's wishes had to be honored. They hoped he understood. Kyle had borrowed some money from them but had quickly gotten a job. He and Jenny were in a small but nice inner city apartment. This wasn't what they'd dreamed of for their son, but they were proud he was handling the situation. They would let Jeff and Cherry know when the baby was born.

Cherry hadn't gone with Jeff on that or any of his quests. She couldn't. It was too humiliating to have others see her as the wicked mother her child so apparently despised. Jenny had been rescued enough. This was one time too many. Her heart was totally broken and she spent nights crying herself to sleep in Jeff's arms, but to give the matter undue outward attention was more than she could bear.

She busied herself by taking a job, leaving the after-school babysitting of the boys to her mother. They could have been left alone if not for the fear Cherry carried of either of them following in Jenny's footsteps. The boys were her remaining life and she needed to be on top of her game unencumbered by concern for their well being. She answered their questions about Jenny, their missing her, their worry, with reassurance that Jenny was fine and must miss them too. The empty words didn't quiet their wondering so Cherry turned to distractions, pushing their activities to a point of near exhaustion for the family. That seemed to work for the boys, Jeff wasn't fazed, and for her it helped keep a few demons from residing in her head.

The beliefs she had always held so dear were the only salvation Cherry could find. She'd done her best, hadn't she? What more could be asked of a person? All she had wanted for Jenny was a sense of stability, the same stability that had served her own youth so well. Cherry didn't question that to be true, and within that framework sought fault with Jenny's lack of acceptance. Hopefully enough had be instilled to bring Jenny back, or at least lead her to a life of following rules. The responsibility that came with being a mother should make Jenny see the way she'd been raised had reasons and eventual benefits. Then she'd see her mother in a new light. It really could work like that.

The stress, the stress just below the surface of denial, left Cherry with mounting aches and pains. Her knees hurt, her fingers felt oddly stiff when waking. The doctor ruled out arthritis, but at that appointment found adult onset diabetes. Along with that, recurring migraines kept her in bed for days, a bout of pneumonia did the same, both serving to give her more downtime to worry and stress. Setting aside the array of common causes, she viewed it all as penance, fought off self care, and stewed instead about Jenny.

It was possible, given life's unfairness, Jenny would never return. If she didn't, would she be okay? Had she been given enough of a background to transform her into a suitable adult? A mother? Would she ever live by the rules? Was it really so bad if she didn't? Cat hadn't, and Cat seemed fine, always the free one who got what she wanted in spite of not earning it in any proper way. Mark too. Mark now had his own company, a pretty wife, oversized house and money. He was still Mark, doing and saying whatever he pleased. Jenny may end up the same. She may somehow grab all the joy in the world that was so elusive to the unlucky. That would be just par. Deep down Cherry half hoped she would.

When Christmas brought each of the boys a personal card from Jenny, minus any return address, the house atmosphere took on a new feel. They were old enough to clearly grasp the intentional absence of one to their parents. They had been told the facts very factually, including the out of wedlock pregnancy but without unnecessary details. The boys had witnessed the ongoing discord for so long, fair assumption said they could fill in the blanks. They had, but not to the extent now indicated.

Each card, with a handwritten note, contained a picture of the new niece, born just weeks before. An early Christmas present, Jenny told her brothers, a gift from above to her and to them. Someday they'd meet her and love her like she did. Her name was Daisy Sun, a beautiful name for a beautiful new soul. The closing was a wish for a good Christmas, with a paper kiss and a hope they were keeping alive great adventures.

That last was a not very subtle way of telling them not to let their parents ruin them. Cherry saw right through it. How sad of Jenny to misinterpret her upbringing. The boys, meanwhile, got the message too. Combined with the fact Jenny had written to them and in honor of her unqualified absence, they set out, each in his own way, to make home life more than ever a challenge. The change was gradual and waited until after Christmas in favor of presents, but once the shift took hold it was unmistakable. Starting in almost unnoticeable doses, pretending not to hear a call to dinner, it quickly turned into outbursts at every parental command. Cherry knew if she didn't act fast, she'd lose her sons too.

In a few quiet moments, when nothing else was to be gained, she gave herself credit for at least giving her children sibling solidarity, even if that came at a price. They had banded without words against her and Jeff, against all of their values and teachings, but mainly just against them. The rest was simply a way to get across the message. They'd concluded Jenny wouldn't have left without good reason, the most obvious being their mother, but their dad should have stepped up to help. He was at fault too. Jenny had to fight back, had to take care of herself. They were doing the same.

By spring, Cherry could take no more. The image of being an ogre was wearing on her patience. That and the fact she ached for Jenny and the granddaughter she'd never seen moved Cherry into action. There was no phone listing – a way to save money or hide – so with just the city to go on, and knowing Kyle had worked his way through high school as an apprentice at the local newspaper, she started calling papers and asked for him. Much to her amazement, on just the third or fourth try, one said he couldn't come to the phone. She thanked them, hung up, and sat there before quickly retracing the number and getting an address. That gave her a likely vicinity, the rest had to be done on foot.

For the next month and more, she shopped every Saturday, or told Jeff she was. He'd want to come along if anything but shopping. She stocked up on groceries at what were probable markets Jenny may frequent, browsed baby stores, malls, and the nearby park. She walked the sidewalk in outward directions from the newspaper company to apartments, scouring the windows of row upon row of tall housing with a hope against logic of Jenny waving. Every window seemed to hold tight secrets, curtains blowing or tightly closed, yells from some, hustle on the streets below. Jenny, her daughter, lived somewhere here in a world apart from all she had known. The mission overrode Cherry's mounting angst.

On a sunny May midmorning, as she approached the park, her eyes combed the benches on the left then shifted to path in front of her. There was Jenny, not more than twenty feet ahead, coming directly toward her, unaware, cooing around the corner of a stroller at her baby. As concretely as Cherry had worked for this moment, it now seemed a total miracle. Her heart raced and her mind went blank. There was no turning back, there was no hiding. Now was the time for the confrontation she'd wanted yet wasn't sure she'd actually expected. Jenny raised her head. As faint smiles covered the panic in both of their faces, they stopped in their tracks, with the baby, the sidewalk, the years of history buffering the air between them.

"This is Daisy." Jenny was the first to speak when closer, reaching around and into the stroller for the baby's hand.

Cherry stepped forward at this apparent permission from Jenny. She flashed a big smile at Daisy, bent to be a bit closer, but was hesitant to reach out for a touch. Daisy had Jenny's eyes, deep wells of superior knowledge, and the same blonde curls. Nick's. Nick had a grandchild too. This wasn't the first time that had crossed her mind, but seeing the baby instantly ignited the fresh legacy bond.

"Could we find a bench to sit for awhile? Catch up a little?" Cherry's voice quivered as she said it, venturing a straight faced look at Jenny, hoping a mother's authority still held.

"I can't stay long. Kyle will wonder where I am."

The unintentional irony of the words hovered in stillness between the two women. Jenny lowered her eyes. Of all of her seemingly outrageous qualities, cruelty was not one of them. This conversation was going to be awkward enough without stooping to low blows.

"There's a spot," Cherry said pointing, a sharp retort silenced at the tip of her tongue. She kept a respectful space between herself and Jenny as they made their way to the empty bench. This had to go well. It just had to.

"She's beautiful," Cherry said with a nod and stare at Daisy in the stroller. She ached to pick her granddaughter up, but that would be left to Jenny, who so far was not making the offer. "How was your delivery?"

"Hurt like hell."

"Jenny, I…"

"Why did you come here?"

"I had to. I just had to. You know how you feel about Daisy? That's how I feel about you. I had to make sure you were okay."

Jenny was determined to not be cajoled. "You can't make me come back, you know."

"I know. I don't intend to."

With that issue so unceremoniously out of the way, it was Jenny who decided to get to the meat. "When Daisy grows up, I'm going to let her be who she wants to be. I'm going to listen to her and teach her to not be afraid of anything, to be curious, to…"

"That's easy to say now. But the first time she's in danger…"

"What danger? Being a kid? Being a person who's different than you?" That had let the real intent fly, not that it had been at all hidden.

"I did my best, Jenny. All I ever wanted for you was to grow up with values, respect, just the normal things any parent wants. I'm sorry if I made mistakes. You will with her too. They just happen."

"See, you still really don't get it. Values, respect. What about individuality? What about showing her how to be happy, that stuff?"

This was leading to the same old rapport that had haunted their relationship from the beginning. Cherry had to think. As much as she felt strongly about her position, and knew no other way, she had to bypass it to find common ground. The future of their family rode on today's outcome. Of that much she had no doubt. Reaching into her memory arsenal of what she so often had wanted from her mother, Cherry rose to the occasion with more grace than she knew she possessed.

"That's all I ever really wanted for you, honey. It really is. I'm sorry I didn't show you that. I didn't know how."

Jenny had never heard such an admission, and was left, for a moment, defenseless. She looked at her mother, hunched and lost in her grief, and in that moment felt connected for the first time she could remember. Motherhood was hard, the responsibilities of it just dawning these last couple months. She had no intention of making the same mistakes, but who knew. Maybe someday Daisy would rebel against her and all that she tried to do. Who knew.

Cherry took a hold of the pause. "If I didn't care so much, it'd have been easy to just let you do whatever. It's complicated, Jen, it's…"

"I know."

Jenny didn't know, not yet, hopefully not ever. Her existence from conception had set in motion a life changing event Cherry could never explain, not in a way that would make it alright. Maybe if she'd been honest from the start, when Jenny could first understand, they wouldn't be sitting here today. Maybe. Maybe it wouldn't have mattered.

"Want to hold Daisy?"

That brought a smile and a loving reach for the baby as Jenny handed her over to the anxious grandmother to cuddle. The conversation turned to Daisy's newest achievement, pulling herself up against furniture. Cherry ached at how much she'd missed, but now wasn't the time to show it.

"How's Kyle?"

"Hates his job. He's going back to school in the fall."

"Where does that leave you?"

"Guess we're going to live with his parents."

Cherry knew not to interject any alternative wishes. "You'll come visit then? The boys would love it! Dad too. They miss you so much. Me too, honey. Me too."

"Sure. Sometime."

Events were to bring that and more to fruition rather soon. When Kyle, exposed to college life, fell in love with someone else, Jenny moved back home with Cherry and Jeff. The stay would be short lived, with independent Jenny, her child in tow, setting out into the world again before long, but for the duration of that particular homecoming, the family seemed a family for one more try.

Mother and daughter, so bound by circumstances seemingly out of their hands, determined to be good parents each at her age, parted that day in the park with a renewed respect that would carry them through the years, just below the words and attitudes that just weren't destined to change.

Chapter 4

Cherry didn't mention Jenny's escapade, the big one or the others, to the Highland girls. The fact she had owned up to Jenny's conception, even though that'd taken years, was all the honesty needed. They then knew her tie with Nick, her ability to get him into bed. That was enough to share. That much gave her the residual effect of additional belonging, too nice to risk losing.

She had surprised herself at that telling, not at all planning to after keeping it silent so long, it had just slipped one reunion from her heart to Sydney with no forewarning. Not more than a month later, Jenny, quietly already pregnant with Daisy, had left home for good. Maybe there had been signs and their pressure had forced out the words. Or maybe the telling was what had prompted Jenny in some kind of roundabout way. Certainly the girls hadn't said anything, so Jenny's running likely was punishment, another punishment, stemming this time from the unloading.

In the years since, though, she did talk to the girls of Daisy with pride, letting only bits of unbecoming circumstances slip here and there. None of it was a lie, she just wasn't telling quite the whole truth. Some things were left better within the confines of family secrets. Jenny was still keeping up her guard, and Cherry and Jeff only got to see Daisy during summer vacations when they made the trek to visit. That didn't stop Cherry from glamorizing the time in between. She didn't do that just for conversation; she needed to convince herself all was well.

Jenny had moved as seemingly far away as she could, flitting from California to Texas to eventually Nevada where she settled with her husband of now seven years. The visits were short, the talk pleasantly reserved, but they solidified a continuing connection. As long as Cherry kept her advice at a minimum, usually an unsuccessful task, things remained open between them.

The other grandchildren too got their doings retold. Bruce had moved to Colorado and so far was unmarried, but Steve and his wife had a boy and girl and lived relatively close to home. The kids were the light of Cherry's life. It went without saying they gave her headaches, and grandma still had all her rules, but the redemption factor the new generation was giving surely had to be God's way of forgiving if by chance she'd ever erred.

"Can't believe Daisy's almost seventeen," Sydney said, fixing corn for that night's boil. "Seems like Jenny was just that age. Where does the time go?"

"Cripe! You sound like an old geezer, Syd," shouted Cat from her dig in the pantry. "In my day I had to walk ten miles to school, uphill both ways…"

"Potatoes!"

Cat emerged with a bucket full. "Here you go, granny. Hey, where's Cherry? I thought she was in here. Need to ask her how freakin' old are we."

Maggie came to raise her glass to clank Cat's. "She's outside. The answer is we're too freakin' old."

Sydney took the potatoes with a roll of her eyes and a snap to Cat's ass with a towel. The preparations done, they headed out to the deck. They'd be holding the reunions here at Sydney's on the beach for so long they hadn't kept count, until just now when they realized this was number twenty five, more in all but the twenty fifth just here on her land. That deserved a toast, a heartfelt thanks to Syd for making these what they were. If they'd continued just meeting at the old restaurant and hotel, they weren't sure they'd have stayed so cohered. These weekends at Syd's had seen their relationship, their lives, and Sydney's house grow and fine tune in maturity.

"That's exquisite, Syd!" Sadie pointed and squirmed for a better view of a half hidden new garden statue. "Where did you find it?"

"We saw one like it in Greece last year, not for sale, so I hunted this one down through my suppliers. Surprised the shit out of me to actually find it," answered Sydney.

Maggie grinned. "Right. Like you'd have stopped before you did."

Settled with their wine and margaritas, the conversation revolved around catching up and commiserating about how fast time had flown. Each had their own way of seeing it, none all that pleased but most taking it in stride. The talk became centered on families, as it had for years, each knowing that the more personal, inner soul reaching discussions would come later at the bonfire with a heavier round of drinks.

"Sometimes it seems that you guys are my only friends, you know? Not that that's bad! It's just that between the kids and grandkids, that's our social life," Cherry said. "Probably is natural, I guess."

"Yeah, I think it is," said Maggie. "Even having the restaurant, we see a lot of people but really don't run around with them. It's the kids, and family stuff. With Angel in the city now, I thought we'd have more time, but all we do is make trips to see her. And go to Jaime's games. That's it."

"You've got us." Sydney pretended to be hurt.

"You don't count. You're like the crazy aunt and uncle every family has. Besides, you're Highland, that was the point."

"How does Angel like her job?" Cat asked. "I still think she and my Jack should get it on."

"She hates it, just can't land one in her field. She thinks she might switch and go to culinary school. She was going to sign up this fall but now thinks she'll wait till mid term. It's weird, she's got so many choices, a lot more than I remember having, but that makes it hard to decide, although finally landing on this one is funny. You'd think it would have been where she'd started."

"She can be the chef at Jack's resort. There you go. Tell her to call him."

Cherry laughed. "Or she could take over her parent's place, goofy."

"Is Diana still with that one boyfriend?" Maggie asked Wren.

"Unfortunately. It's not that I don't like him, she's just too young to be that involved. I thought starting college would help. But she just doesn't want to look around."

"He can hear, right?" Cherry said. "Isn't that good? I mean, if they both couldn't…"

"Yeah, he can, but that's not an issue as much as whether or not he's right for her. I want her to kind of check out the field, you know?"

Sydney got up for more wine. "You think it could be just sex? If they are?"

"Oh, I know they are. She's proud of it. I'm glad she's so open, and she's responsible about it and all, but still…"

"Still, she's getting more than her mom!" That was Cat's way of asking.

Wren just smiled her pretty, shy smile, and gave a shrug that said maybe or not. Cat knew her too well.

"You dog, you! You are! Wren's getting la-id, Wren's getting la-id," sang her voice nearly in tune.

"Is it still called getting laid when we're this old?" Sydney was always stoic in approach. "Don't we make love now, or have a romantic encounter or something?"

"It was always making love for me," Maggie said. "Almost always, anyway."

Cat was sincerely puzzled. "What does age have to do with it? It's still the same thing. It's still getting it on! It's still grabbing a piece. It's…"

"So, then, I grabbed a piece last night if anybody wanted to know," Sydney said, trying out the phrase in perspective. "Still's good, that's all I know."

"See," said Sadie. "That just doesn't sound right, I don't think. But how come? How come it's different?"

Cherry was sure she knew. "Because she's married. Married sex is different. It's sacred."

Cat couldn't wait to jump all over that one. "Yeah, well, there you go. That's why sex dies. Gotta keep it fun, gotta keep it kinda dirty. That's sacred, baby. Really opening up to someone is holy. Works for me. Joe loves it when I…"

"You guys are still in the newlywed stage, sort of. That's all," Cherry argued. "You just wait."

"We're way past newlyweds. Five, no, six years already."

"Try thirty five, then talk to me."

"Don't you plan on being long gone by then?"

A hush fell. They all knew Cat's intent, she'd been using this tactic on Cherry ever since Cherry first aired, among her other worries, a dire prediction of dying young, and whether or not it was working, it left an uncomfortable air. They knew, though, Cat was coming from a place that was hurting as much as they were at the thought, if not even more in the strange connection she had with Cherry. Cherry's fear of an early death, not seeming serious until recent years, was not something any could handle. At least Cat was trying, if probably in a wrong way.

"You'd like that, wouldn't you? Maybe I'll stick around just to piss you off."

Then again, maybe Cat's method had merit.

"That's my girl! Hey, forgot to tell you guys Jack's got a new girlfriend." Cat knew exactly what she was doing in taking the focus off Cherry. "Fin-a-ly! He's been so wrapped up in the resort stuff I was beginning to wonder if his thing had dried up or what."

"Geez, Cat! Did you say that to him?" Maggie was laughing as she said it, never yet always surprised by what flew out of Cat.

"Yeah. I said he'd better use it or lose it. Have to lay it on the line with these kids. Not that he's a kid any more. And not that he has to get married or anything, I just could tell he was kind of worrying about it himself. Once he took the time out to think about it."

"You and Joe think about ever moving closer to him?" Sydney asked.

"Maybe to retire, but not now. Joe loves him like I do, and the place is gorgeous, so relaxing, but we both are way too busy yet to think about it."

"It's not all that far off," Sadie said. "Retirement, I mean."

The responses were a mix that boiled down to the type of work one was doing. Sixty two wasn't old age anymore, and especially not from their vantage point of fifty seven. Maggie and Jay would likely stay with the restaurant until one of the kids showed interest one way or another. Sydney's self employed design work could continue until she tired of it, which was not in the foreseeable future, and Sadie, who had brought it up and had two published books under her belt, the second just this year, had no plans to ever retire.

"No ring around your neck yet from your Sam?" Cat asked her.

"Nope. Sam's great, he really is, as a boyfriend, or whatever it's called at this age. I just like things the way they are."

"Speaking of getting laid," Sydney chuckled with a glance at Cat. "Wrennie. Let's get back to what's up with you."

"Yeah, Wren! You never spilled!" Cat squealed.

"Well, no ring around my neck either. I'm pretty sure I don't ever want there to be one, pretty sure, anyway. He's a great guy, I met him doing a consult for his company. He's been divorced for about fifteen years. And likes it, being single. But he also likes me. Very much, it seems. We'll see. We just started, have only seen him once outside of work, haven't even slept together yet, so who knows."

"Name. We need a name," Cherry teased.

"Adam. Adam Love." She caught the looks. "I'm serious. That's cross-my-heart his name."

The funny taunts about his name and the newness of Wren's excitement brought a youthful lift to the group, overriding gray hair and wrinkles. None were visibly gray, none planned on stopping the dye, but this talk gave an internal match to the vision they still held of themselves when not studying their faces in a mirror. They were once again, if only for this afternoon on the deck, a group of giddy girls back at school.

The feeling tided them into Saturday, but waking sensibly without hangovers and then calls to home reminded them once again of the difference. They lolled on the porch after breakfast, choosing camaraderie over activities, although the beach looked inviting for a later swim.

"Syd and I had our fortieth high school reunion this summer. You guys go to yours?" Maggie asked.

"I did," said Sadie. "Just last weekend. It was a blast. Pretty good turnout, I suppose because it's kind of a landmark one. Man, there's such a difference in people. Some seemed so old! Chronic this, chronic that. Already! But the good thing was it seemed like no one put on pretenses anymore. That was cool."

"Run into anybody interesting?" Cherry wanted to know.

"Guys? No, not really. For one, I took Sam with me. Kind of hard to rekindle old junk when you bring a date."

Sydney had caught Cherry's drift. "I think she meant Nick."

"Oh yeah," Sadie said, looking from her to Cherry. "I mean, no. He wasn't there. I did see Ken Jacobs, he and Nick pretty much ran our class, and he said he sees Nick every once in awhile. All's well, that's about all he said."

Talk of Nick, even when it came to Sydney's after college relationship with him, had been kept to a minimum since Cherry's admission of him fathering Jenny. The fact Cherry still refused to tell Jenny had become a sore spot of sorts, so it seemed best to not venture near. As much as they respected her decision, and could see a bit her point, in their opinion honesty was always the best policy. Telling would be hard, the hardest thing Cherry might ever do, but Jenny deserved to know and, in the end, would quite likely respect Cherry more for having the courage to face it. That might be true if she'd done so early on, said Cherry. Each passing year the odds had diminished until the chance seemed just too late to take.

Within her diverse personality traits, Cherry was a hilarious story teller, and to cover the uneasiness at the mention of Nick, even though she'd brought it up, she launched into one using seemingly real teenage friends of her granddaughter, tying in to the talk of high school. "So this girl Marcy says, 'Either tell your mom hook-up can mean something different or don't let her talk to mine! I'm grounded for a year!'" Cherry got the round of laughs she'd wanted.

The gift was a talent she'd relies on so much lately. It covered for others, along for herself, the fears that were attempting to overtake her. Humor had been the one thing she used when the fears were personal and couldn't be calmed by self control. As much as she could put on a front at this reunion, the wrenching innocence of those days had recently felt completely gone. These new fears were all too valid.

The girls hadn't mentioned 9/11 this time. They had the year after and a bit the one following, but since had let it drop. They seemed secure. So did almost everyone else. It boggled Cherry that five years time could remove the terror so completely. The news, the government, kept it alive, but that seemed to be all who cared. People were going on with their lives. She had too, for the sake of her family, but the threat of danger loomed in the recesses of her mind, never far from the surface and in the shape of her thoughts. The frightening state of the world, as she saw it, was a sign her long held beliefs were true. A person had to be on guard, any moment or the next it all could be gone. There were times she found herself thinking it could be almost a blessing to have it over, just have it end. That would stop the worry. Yet she clung in fear of that very thing happening. It was so hard being her in her head.

It was depression, the doctor had said, and treated her for it along with the diabetes and more recent kidney trouble. He said depression after 9/11 affected mainly those directly involved but others too, so she wasn't alone. Having a name for it didn't erase reality or the pain she'd felt for so long. Losing her mother had perhaps been the beginning. The loss was still daily painful even after the length of these years. The ramifications were even more so. Or maybe it'd started with Jenny. Her leaving, her antics. Her existence. At least the meds now brought some relief.

"I need a walk," Cat said, standing to stretch. "So do you there, Blossom. Let's hit the trail."

The others agreed a little movement was needed. They paired off, Maggie and Wren for a walk on the beach and Sadie asking Sydney for another tour of the back gardens.

"So catch me up," Cat said as they settled on a cliff edge by the woods. "You haven't called much lately. How's things?" It seemed wise to not add that Sadie had tipped to some trouble. Ganging up was not likely to work.

"Oh, fine. The doctors aren't real thrilled with my numbers, the kidney, diabetes stuff, but I'm hanging in there. Other than that, good, I guess."

"Bullshit," Cat said, reaching over to tickle Cherry's side, finally resting her hand on her friend's shoulder. "Bullshit, bullshit, bullshit."

"Cat, you just don't..." But the humanity of the touch, the tenderness and closeness of it, almost brought Cherry to tears. This was a side to their relationship the quibbling disguised.

"What? Don't get it? Not if you don't talk to me, I don't."

"It's nothing."

Cat just sat with her hand still in place.

"It's everything, you know. Just everything. The whole world's a mess, my life's a mess. I tried, I really did my best, with the kids, with Jenny, and I'd do it all the same again but it just didn't end up like it should have. None of it. I don't get it. So you can't get it if I even can't."

"I'm sure I can't, but if you talk out loud, I bet you can."

Talking was the one thing Cherry so desperately needed to do. Talk and be heard. She couldn't do it with Jeff, she'd tried, he just wanted to comfort her with empty, side-tracking words. She certainly couldn't share any of this with the kids, if any would have listened at all, they were the ones she wanted to protect. There was no one else in her life that cared. Cat. Cat cared.

The two women, one's glass always half empty, the other relentlessly half full, in their unfathomable and raucous link, had been there for each other since first meeting. It had been Cherry that Sydney called on to be the one to reach Cat when Cat lost Rocky. Rocky had been more than a husband, a husband in the sense of Jeff, he'd been Cat's mentor and full fledged partner and his death had been too much to grasp. Cherry, bless her heart, had gotten Cat through it. She'd given it all she had and didn't quit, she kept pounding away, until Cat grabbed a hold. Cherry had dug in and came out with every ounce of strength and wisdom she had, wisdom that countered Cat's but was so perfectly needed and worked.

Now Cat had to do the same. Whatever Cherry's situation was, and Cat had suspicious clues, it was different yet much the same. There was a looming despair to Cherry, a dying of the Cherry she knew. There was the worry of an actual early death like her mother, Cat knew about that, but the feeling in the pit of Cat's stomach said it was something else or something more. Cherry just had to talk her way to its core.

Cherry began. "Like I said, it's everything. It's like everything in Revelations is… right on our doorstep." She had a hard time just saying the words as if they might bring their truth closer. "I know you don't believe any of that, but even so, look at 9/11. I mean, you can't disagree with that…"

Cat had learned long ago not to argue religious beliefs with Cherry, sporting as it could be. Throwing 9/11 into the mix gave her an honest out. "Who's disagreeing? I know that stuff is scary."

"Saying scary is like saying chocolate tastes kinda good."

The chuckle from both helped at the moment, but Cat didn't want this brushed under the rug. She could tell Cherry was close to finding the words needed. That little joke was a way of stalling.

The words were starting to come. "Cat, you know how, when

Rocky died, when you went to the hospital and saw him like that? It's okay to say this, isn't it?"

"Of course. What about it?"

"It's just that I remember going too, to see my mother. I thought she'd be sitting up in bed or something when I got there, and I went as soon as my dad called, but by the time I got there she was gone. Just that fast. She'd been fine the day before. The next she was gone."

"Oh yeah, don't have to tell me. Same thing with Rocky. It's almost impossible to deal with, to get."

Cherry turned to face her. "It is. It's impossible, Cat. I just can't stand that life is so… fragile, you know?"

"What I know is that until it happened to Rocky, I didn't get how much you went through with your mom's death. I'm sorry, sweetie. I remember you seemed okay, the things you said about it being life and all…"

"I had to say that stuff, for the kids. I guess for me too. I was trying to convince myself."

"I think for me, after that, I think I turned into a happier person. I don't mean not having Rocky, shit no. And not right away, guess I don't have to tell you that, I mean eventually seeing how precious time is. What a gift it is."

"Sounds like a poster or something."

"It's all I got. But it's the truth. A real, real truth. Seriously. I know you're worried about going young like your mother…"

"And aunt."

Cat took a breath. "Didn't you tell me your aunt had cancer? And your mom's was heart failure? Blossom! There's no linking thread there! I wish you'd see that, I wish there was something I could do to change your mind about all that."

"It's not my mind, it's physical."

"Wrong!" It didn't seem productive to debate it, years of such talk had proven fruitless, still Cat had to try. "What would it hurt to keep telling yourself you're fine, you're going to live to a hundred, and maybe throw in something about enjoying every minute of it while you're at it?"

"To tell you the truth, I might not even care about going if…."

She stopped. Cat stopped. This was the nitty-gritty and there was no way Cat was going to interfere. A long moment passed.

Cat, despite her post grad education in the psychology of natures, had never fined tuned her patience. She soon couldn't, opting for a chance good judgment, stand the wait.

"If what, sweetie? Is it about Jenny?"

Cherry flashed the briefest look of surprise before her thoughts rearranged. "Cat, you still think I should tell her, even after all this time?"

"Yes. Now give me the real scoop." Nothing slipped by Cat.

Cherry, now too afraid, had to change the angle of where she had headed this. "You just said it. I'm having second thoughts about that. I've been second guessing it since I got pregnant with her. I don't know, I just don't know."

It was obvious to Cat Cherry was playing coy, her seeming openness a diversion from something more pressing. But to prod might shut her down completely.

"Okay, let's go over the pros and cons. Jenny's an adult now, she's a mother, she could see it from that perspective, you know, a mother's love. Protection. She's maybe had questions all along, just intuitive stuff, so knowing could make her feel very relieved to have that answered."

Cat had a point, the only point Cherry had let enter her mind these past few years. It would feel good, before death came, to set things straight with Jenny. Jenny's troubles could have been due to some inkling of not fully belonging, not in the way they'd pretended. Still, Jenny might take it wrong, she might totally take away the bit of love she had. Dying would be extra horrible then. For that and other reasons, Cherry knew the debate was useless. She'd go to her grave with the secret.

"Something to think about anyway," Cat was saying. "So, what else is bugging that twisted brain of yours?"

"You, at the moment." Cherry stood to leave, giving Cat a light smack on the head. She'd really needed to tell Cat, to have Cat's help. She even had planned the words. But she just couldn't. This was too big. Of all the things that scared her, this one was the most immediately dangerous. She'd have to present it very carefully. Cherry had lost her nerve.

They rejoined the others, Cat fully aware she may have blown it with Cherry but, at the same time, was a firm believer that things happen as they should. Cherry needed to talk on Cherry's terms, when she was ready. Whatever the problem was, it was apparently keeping her from calling it quits. So that was good. No way was this dying young shit going to fly.

By the Sunday goodbyes, the six were renewed for another year. The reunion had been, as always, great fun with terrific food, conversation, and tidbits of shared wisdom on each passing stage. Much of the talk during Saturday night's dinner had centered on Maggie's mother living now with her and Jay, just one of the changing issues coming to light as the years were so subtly transforming them. While together, although each saw in the other the toll of time, a reflection of her own mortality, it still seemed the world was alright. They could be nineteen again and fifty seven at the same time. Only the growing melancholy of the goodbyes gave any hint of the truth they accepted.

"Car's all packed. You ready?" Sadie asked Cherry.

"No!" Cherry laughed and went for one more round of hugs, giving Cat an extra hard squeeze. In the last few years, each parting for Cherry had a sense of perhaps being the last, if not the last then for sure close to it. This one brought tears to her eyes.

"I'll call," she whispered to Cat.

"You better or I'll hunt you down and it won't be pretty."

That was friendship.

Chapter 5

Everyone had a right to some secrets, Cherry was convinced of that, it was part of life and there wasn't a person alive who didn't have something to hide. She'd come to accept the origin of Jenny as one of those. It had held this far and no one, unless maybe Jenny, seemed the worse for the withholding. Cat and the others weren't aware of the difficulty involved in coming clean, as they put it. No, that secret could stay hidden. This other, however, could not.

Cherry had never, almost never, thought of it as embezzling. Embezzling was stealing. All she had done was simply take what was due her without asking. The difference was huge, they were two separate things. She'd told herself that every time she did it.

Glenn Griffin was a schmuck, there was no doubt about that. She'd worked for him long enough to have figured that out, in fact, it'd only taken a couple weeks. The quarters were tight in the Griffin Insurance Agency, tight with paper thin walls, and Cherry, at her post as receptionist, caught on without meaning to suspect. Her multi-task roll doing payroll checks and typing up client forms confirmed it. Glenn Griffin was using every loophole he could to stay just a hair within the letter of the law.

She would hear him on the phone, so casually, so neighborly, convincing an elderly couple to take out exorbitant coverage. She'd hear him laughing with either of his agents, both obviously of his ilk, after successful days of overcharges and too easy, erroneous sells. And she saw it in the scribbled notes he'd give her to calculate pay for those same agents. He was even cheating them. Substantial as their checks were, they were shorted each week by deducting undetectable fees. Charges for printed material. A flat, undefined overhead contribution. Never to be noted, of course. Never itemized. Just part of the practice of business.

The paycheck issue might have passed as acceptable if the agents hadn't one day questioned their checks within earshot. They dismissed the small doubt, assuring each other Glenn was a straight shooter, their buddy and decent boss. He'd rape clients, that with a laugh, but he'd be honest with them. They let it go, never suspecting the receptionist heard or had cared, or that a crime spree was subconsciously taking root in her head.

If Glenn had been fairer with her pay, it may not have sprung into action, but unfortunately he seemed to be cheating her too. Her first review came and went with a simple 'good job, kiddo' along with additional work. She now could be trusted with bank runs and handling the petty cash. The next review brought a nickel raise, due to the fine quality of her work, he said, seeming to think she'd be pleased. She wasn't, but smiled a polite thank you to him.

After that there were no more reviews, just randomly small increases and token Christmas bonuses. Cherry had become a part of the team, doing her job with no need to be supervised or cajoled. With all the problems at home, she let her grievances fade into the background and made the job, tedious as it was, an escape. And the money it brought in helped supplement the family budget. She and Jeff had quickly become dependent on it, so to quit was out of the question. Cherry adapted and accepted it as part of life's unfairness.

And then there was Glenn. As slimy as he was on the inside, outside he was charming, rather good looking, and his smooth way of talking clients into buying what they didn't need worked as well on Cherry. That led for her to a heavy hint of sexual tension that persisted despite all she knew to be true of him. It kept her there although, in her seventeen years with him, she'd seen him through two wives with not the slightest of actual advances toward her either when he was married or not. It somehow didn't deter her from a slight thrill in his presence. It made the job bearable.

It gave her an emotion to feel.

For all of his tight fisted financial ways, Glenn wasn't interested in the petty operations of the company. Those details he left to Cherry. He was too busy pocketing inflated portions of premiums and rounding up new clients to snag. Cherry paid the bills, maintained the records, kept the files in order and answered the phone. At her first review back in the beginning, she'd even been given the rubber stamp to sign checks. She handled everything not directly involved in signing a client's policy. Glenn assumed she was doing a good job.

So it wasn't hard for Cherry, although still nerve-wracking, to start on her path as a felon. The first time didn't occur until well into a year on the job. The death of her mother, so unexpected, such a bottomless loss, threw Cherry into an excruciating fog. She couldn't come in to work, she told Glenn by phone. He understood, but was it possible she stop by to just finish payroll, then take as many days as she needed. Cherry agreed through her tears.

As she finished the work and was tucking the ledger in its drawer, there it was. The petty cash envelop. She had been blindly scouring her closet the night before to find a decent dress for the funeral. The closest she could come to one that was dark was a royal blue pantsuit a good size too small. She counted the bills and the change. Of its sixty four ninety, she slid two twenties and a ten into her purse. She'd pay it back later.

With every intent to do just that, she left that day for the store, fifty dollars richer. She was able to bypass the small slam against her ingrained morality, and what her mother would have thought, by telling herself the dress was vital. She had to honor her mother the very best she could. It would be highly inappropriate for the daughter of the deceased to appear in inappropriate clothes. It wasn't stealing, it was borrowing. There was nothing at all wrong with that.

She replaced the fifty in two parts over the next month's pay periods. It cut into the groceries, but it was important to get it done before Glenn noticed. Not that he ever looked. Petty cash was her domain, used for supplies only she knew were needed. She'd meticulously kept slips of anything spent, but when forgotten, had implanted a handwritten note. Glenn found that habit, and the fact she'd run it by him, bothersome. Petty was petty, after all. No need to care about petty.

After the ease of her first mishandling, the tempting sight of cash sitting uselessly in the drawer was too much. A few dollars here and there for lunch treats on awful days became justified and not necessarily repaid. Glenn owed her for all she did. And that little truth, in its unprecedented logic, began to have a mind of its own, soon to become Cherry's new and improved gospel version of choice.

Petty cash was just the first step. After running short one day at the grocery store and having to put two items back, it occurred to her a cost of living raise was not too much to ask, barring the fact she just couldn't. Minimum wage had recently taken a jump and, although she was already slightly above that, she certainly deserved much more. She was a college graduate. Granted, the job didn't require a rocket science degree, but it did call on her experience and aptitude. It wasn't just deserving, it was needing, that justified her call to action.

She began padding her check with gas expense for errands, supplies she brought from home, and extra time for working into her lunch hour when a form required immediate attention. None of that combined amounted to noticeable increases, five or ten dollars at most, and always in odd cents with explanations to back up each one. Glenn would likely never check, but if he did, she'd have an answer ready.

He wasn't, however, she was sure, in a position to challenge her. He had always seemed to suspect she wasn't blind to his ways, but one day they'd mutually erased any doubt and worry. As he told her how to record a misappropriated claim, without any intentional thought on her part she'd given him just the slightest of looks. He looked back, a flash of alarm and then a wink. She smiled. That's all it took to create alliance. While various agents came and went, she and Glenn Griffin evolved into a team unto themselves.

He needed her as a discreet secretary as much as she needed the job, and the eventual comfort and free rein of the books kept her there without deep-seated qualms. By the time she'd begun padding her paycheck she'd quit snitching the petty cash and had restocked it dollar by dollar to the best of her memory. That seemed the honest thing to do despite the fact taking it hadn't really felt wrong.

Glenn didn't mention her justified pay increases until several months after she'd started taking them. He'd noticed her check atop her purse and asked with a laugh if she'd put in overtime or what.

She could have agreed, or told him the truth, pulling out one of her explanations, but Cherry wasn't that bold or fast on her feet when caught off guard with a face to face. He was still her boss, and even with the goods she had on him and the likelihood of her excuses passing, a confrontation suddenly felt risky.

"New tax tables, she stammered. "I changed my exemptions," an alternative that had just popped to the forefront. For all of her rigidity about certain ethics, Cherry had grown to have nothing against lying when done in the name of self preservation. Taking without asking fell under that too.

Glenn shrugged with a wink, an open-to-interruption wink. His faith in the loyal, church-going Cherry had not let an alternative exist.

In the beginning he would have been right, but something in Cherry had given way over the years, swaying her from the principles she'd once held so dear. It wasn't visible, it didn't seem huge, she still maintained the core and roots of most values, but it was altering enough to change her. It grew seemingly without her permission until the self deceit had attached itself comfortably along side her staunch and rigid beliefs. For as long as she needed to continue the charade, Cherry was fine with its rightness.

On the surface, the death of her mother had been the cause of this loosening. Life had taken unfairness one step too far. That unlucky feeling, so long held, so practiced, had finally pushed and pulled until Cherry felt no choice but to fight back. That stance, as the pilfering evolved, gave her something she'd not experienced. Retaliation. Revenge. A foreign sense of pride, twisted but alive unhindered. She had unwittingly put herself in the position of first needing then getting used to the extra money as necessary, to then having it satisfy a hunger she just couldn't name.

Her mother had been her rock, her constant companion over even Jeff. She'd turned to her mother for help with everyday life, and for reinforcement of beliefs when needed. Her mother was her best friend. They had daily morning coffee until Cherry started work, a ritual that had sustained Cherry through the long years of turbulence. Without her, Cherry was still lost.

There'd been no forewarning of that call from her dad. Her mom had collapsed after doing dishes; he'd called an ambulance and didn't have time to notify anyone else until at the hospital where things got so blurry. Cherry and Jeff met him there in time to hear the doctor going over the details. Her dad had done a fine job, he said, he should be proud he'd acted so fast, but when it was massive like this, there was nothing anyone could do. With heartfelt sympathies, he turned and left them to their grief.

Cherry functioned as the oldest child during the initial aftermath days, helping her father cope, notifying relatives and taking care of funeral arrangements according to the wishes her parents had planned. Mark soon came, of course, and did what he could, unfamiliar now with the home and people he'd left. He brought his wife and children, the children cousins to hers but virtual strangers. He and Cherry talked of the shame of that, and resolved to change it as circumstances allowed. That likely would never happen.

Not until routine life returned did the full loss of her mother hit Cherry. The routine was what she missed. No more nightly phone calls to discuss the day's events. Sunday dinners with just her father, now coming to her and Jeff's house, screamed the absence of the woman who'd done most of the cooking with such an innate flare. Cherry had learned a great deal watching, helping, but no one could cook like her mother. Not just the food but the empty presence talked more than if she'd been there.

As often as Cherry had been tempted, she'd never confided Jenny's truth to her mother. The omission in hindsight seemed such a deception, a block at this point to letting go of the grief. But her mother's assured disappointment in her, as well as certain disapproval, had always made it too scary to risk. It'd have spoiled all the good they'd spent years and years honing. That really didn't excuse the fact she had owed it to their relationship. The time had just never seemed right. Now it was too late.

That somehow still didn't translate into the benefit of leveling with Jenny.

A full year passed with the grief easing but not fading far from Cherry's thoughts. She was in no frame of mind to think of much else until one of weekly trips to the cemetery brought more. At first she simply placed flowers on the grave, this time to mark the first year anniversary, and held her usual one sided conversation.

Her father's unused marker sat next to her mother's, and scattered under the tree lined rows were those of each parent's families. Her grandparents, great grandparents, great uncles and aunts. Her mother's younger sister, Marcia. Cherry roamed the history before her.

Jed and Hazel, her mother's parents, lay side by side in a spot Cherry knew as a teenager. It had been so sad for her mother, just as it had been for her, to visit and say her piece. Cherry read the inscriptions and dates. Yes, that would have put her at fourteen, her mental math told her. Seventeen when her grandfather joined his wife. She wondered how long her own father would carry on without his. He certainly wasn't old by today's standards, but heartbreak knew no age.

Her grandparents had passed away rather young, she noticed now through adult eyes. And Marcia. Marcia had been fifty four. She had been definitely too young. Her death had been just ten years ago, still fresh and vivid in its senseless taking. So painful for everyone, so sad. Cancer. So scary. Cherry said a prayer against it for herself and her kids as she made her way to her car.

She didn't remember how she got home that day. Fear had gripped her at the cemetery exit. Longevity didn't run in her family. On either parent's side. It had seemed, as a child, that most had been old. They weren't, especially and oddly, too oddly, the women. And her own mother, whom she so closely genetically resembled, from size and shape to spooning fingernails and straight eyelashes, had been only fifty eight. The fact the deaths all had various causes simply reinforced the ill fate in store. Why would she be different? Something would get her, she didn't know what, nor did it matter. She had come from unhealthy stock. The facts were plain. She wasn't long for this world.

It wasn't fair. It was the epitome of unfairness. Tears streamed down her face and she had to pull over before she went off the road. She sat as the world caved in around her. The dash of her car, the steering wheel in the grip of her hands, the trees out the window, the familiarity of all earthly things would be gone. Jeff would be sad. He'd probably remarry. The new wife might be what she never was. The kids would love their new mom. The thoughts just wouldn't stop. She'd never grow old, she'd never get to finish life like other people. She pounded the steering wheel. It just wasn't fair.

By the time she got home, unable to fully accept the scare, her mind had stepped in to shelter her. There were such advancements in medicine. She may be working herself up for nothing. The chill, though, the hair standing on end, reminded her to face reality. Her fate had just been laid out for her, a forewarning to give her time to prepare. Not everyone had that chance. Maybe she was lucky. Ha! Wasn't that just fitting! She sat in the garage and bawled.

She did her best in the days that followed to chalk off the idea as absurd, but days turned to weeks without it diminishing. There were times she could put it aside, occupied by day to day life. More often she could not. Then there were other times when it somehow, in the strangest of ways, jelled into a comfort. She was one in a line of admirable people, all with a destiny obediently fulfilled. When those moments of solace overrode the anguish, Cherry felt mature in accepting the end. It joined her to her mother, her aunt. Her grandparents. And although she didn't know yet, the untimely death of her father ahead by only years, no matter that his was through suicide, would cement that feeling since by then no other could allow her to exist. Death should be considered a blessing of sorts, the kind a person blindly takes with faith. Besides, life was so hard, so often joyless; the hereafter had to be better.

She couldn't explain, even to herself, how or when the knowledge that had taken hold on that day became neither questioned nor denied. In spite of early efforts to rationalize with logic, just as she did with the pay, she finally accepted an early demise as a fact written in stone. If the premonition hadn't made sense in her buried deep recesses, it may have been more conquerable. Instead it answered questions she hadn't known she had. All of her worries, her religious bend, had likely been trying to point her to this. She had to simply accept it. She wondered if that was rationalizing too.

She didn't share her fear with Jeff at first, and never in any depth. He didn't want her to think or say anything about death and dying. The girls knew. She had to talk to someone. They understood to a point and that helped. What they didn't know, what didn't have words, was the conflict of rage and honor within her. Even if it was probably several years off, and even if it was

God's will, the thoughts, especially at night, of leaving Jenny, the boys, the grandchildren as they came along, tormented her into near madness.

The fear took its toll. Even though she put on a brave face and often pushed fear under the rug, she began to grow accustomed to fully using the tools she'd already honed so well. An eye for eye fight surged within her. She hated the world, hated it for all it hadn't given. If life wasn't going to be on her side, she'd take what she wanted to spite it. The combat was not against death, but against the emptiness of living. Cherry was, and always had been, first and foremost a fighter. This was the fight of her life.

And that was how, as the years wore on, cheating Glenn became so easy.

Chapter 6

When Sadie had first moved to the area, Cherry was elated but leery. So much of what went on in life was private, and to have a Highland sister near who might see through was daunting. There hadn't, however, been cause for worry. The twenty or so minute drive that separated them proved to be a substantial deterrent from dropping in on one another, as did Sadie's personality. It just wasn't her style to intrude.

Months went by as Sadie settled into her new surroundings. Cherry drove over to help on more than one occasion, but once done, time passed as their lives were busy. What a shame, both said, to be so close yet let circumstances rule, so eventually they set aside time for a monthly lunch. Of all in the group, the two had had the least interchange on Highland, getting along but coming from different outlooks, so the lunches became a meeting of new friends in all the ways that counted.

Sadie had always been rather quiet, not shy but not one to draw attention. Her focus seemed to be on boys, a Rick in particular for much of the time, and music. She also gravitated to Cat, Cat's causes and way of thinking, interests Cherry found boorish and idealistic at best. Sadie never riled her or got on her nerves, in fact, she had often come to Cherry's rescue when Cat pushed things too far. That seemed to be the extent of what they ever, until lunches, had in common.

Cat and Sadie had remained close over the years, joined by their quest for life's answers. Both were finding them in her own way, each different but agreeing on reasons. Sadie brought that same search to lunch, confiding in Cherry the struggle. Cherry, in turn, reciprocated with the essence of hers. The trust born at Highland gave freedom to their talks, though neither woman did full disclosure. They seemed to understand without words where the line was drawn, in the name of keeping a forever friendship.

Longstanding as their relationship was, Cherry was intimidated during the first solo meetings with the pint sized Sadie who apparently had every advantage. Even after divorcing her famous and runaround husband, Sadie's pampered-life look and confident air remained. But Cherry was to quickly learn that was only the surface. Sadie was still searching for meaning, for answers, happy but unsettled as ever with her stance in life. That set the tone for a mutually serving and wonderfully pleasant camaraderie.

They didn't agreed on everything, or even most, yet the respectful exchange of ideas made the pairing work. Sadie saw beneath Cherry's meticulously woven cover of strength a heart of gold, a tender vulnerability, and the best of intent. She admired that. Cherry loved that Sadie asked her opinion and seemed to take her responses seriously into consideration. Sadie had led such a fascinating life and was again now with her writing, so the fact she had, and openly shared, common human problems was surprising and brought an equality to the table that Cherry relished. She was thankful initial envy hadn't stood in the way.

Their similarities allowed Sadie to see and to counter Cherry's generally pessimistic approach with an understated optimism. She held her own, sympathizing but kindly offering alternatives, especially when it came to the death issue. Sadie knew more of it than any in the group, having eventually listened through countless lunches to the fear in Cherry and the anger. As sure as Sadie was it was all in her head, she also knew that could be where the danger lay. She took on the work of dismantling the idea, fruitless as it might be, and thought some headway was happening until one fateful lunch.

Cherry had realized on the ride home from the last reunion that to confide in Sadie might be the best way to not only alleviate the mental burden that had grown unbearable to carry alone, but to possibly get concrete help. Sadie, her now dearest friend, was trustworthy and close to Cat. Cat was the one with money. The other girls had some too, but Cat was the one most likely to spare it secretly and without condemnation. How Cherry wished it'd never come to this.

As close as she'd come to talking directly to Cat, letting Sadie in on it was scarier so Cherry stalled as long as she could. The reality of Cat and Sadie talking was a given, regardless of which one she approached, and going to Sadie herself rather than behind her back seemed the right decision. That wasn't her hesitancy. She was confident of Cat's opinion; Cat had shared enough of her own inner demons to make that not a problem, but what would Sadie think of her? Was it fair to put Sadie in the middle and hope she'd pick up on the relay without being asked? Would Sadie feel used? Sadie was by now a half successful author; she may unwittingly look down from that stance on something like this. There had to be another way out of this whole mess but none came to mind. Time was closing in, not just for a multitude of personal reasons but one very practical one too.

Still, it took months of lunches and the holidays to pass before the words would come.

"Cherry! Sweetie! How did all this happen?"

"I can hardly believe I did it either. It's a long story, I feel so horrible. It felt like the right thing to do because I needed it and sleazy Glenn was being unfair. I always planned to put it all back, and at first I did. It just got out of hand. I quit doing it about two years ago, my dad dying just did something to me, and started paying it back again. I can't do much at a time, though. I feel awful. You've got to be so disappointed in me."

Sadie had no idea if she was or wasn't. Love and concern overrode, along with the necessity for answers. "Don't worry about me, we just have to think this through. Does this Glenn have any idea you've done this?"

"No. And yes. Probably. Not the dummy account part, but the expenses, the ones I just added on my paychecks, those I've had a feeling he knew about, not in the beginning but after a while. He had to know. He hasn't ever said anything, I'm sure he's afraid if he does I'll blow the whistle on him."

It'd become such a game over the years, if not subliminally from nearly the start. She pretended she didn't know what he was doing, and he turned his back on the pay for her silence. But, clever as he was, he had no idea how much that had cost him.

The dummy accounts, five in all, had been set up per his instructions to shelter his ill-gained excess from taxes. Not that he ever directly said that. Each of the five was noted as a trust under his name and that of an assuredly fictitious client. Cherry was to take what he gave her in usually cash, plus what she withheld from the agents, along with miscellaneously scattered extras from who-knew-what or where, and divvy it into the dummies. He made it sound completely legitimate, fully knowing she by then didn't care.

Shorting the dummies was not brain surgery. She'd do all but one exactly as told, the next time making sure to choose another, so if he was to look, he'd see the majority of all were just right and not question her. That was especially important after the office switched to computerized record keeping. Twenty out here, ten out there, untraceable, unnoticed, but over time substantially adding up to grand theft.

"Cher, okay, first, let's take the expense portions out of the mix. If he never said anything, and you think he knew, that really can't be counted, do you think?"

"Well, maybe not technically, but it matters to me. I just have to pay him back."

Sadie had another question, and no delicate way to put it. "What I don't understand, sweetie, is if you did it, and it felt okay, why is it bothering you now?"

It crossed Cherry's mind to make something up, but this was Sadie, who had become such a wonderful, confiding friend. Sadie, of all the girls, had been empathetic of the underlying issue at hand, although beneath the compassion was possibly a growing boredom and silent disbelief of its depth. Still, having finally worked up the courage to come this far after the past few years of wanting the help, it was only right, in her final mission of extricating her soul, to tell Sadie the truth.

"I know, it's funny, isn't it? I mean, not funny – at all, but weird. All those years, I just blew it off like all I was doing was taking what was mine, you know? But lately, I don't know, it's just different. I've been looking at it differently, now that time… now that I'm getting older."

"If you're going to say…"

"I know you guys don't like it when I talk about it, but to me, it's real. I'm not kidding. I can't help it."

The death thing. Sadie, for as much as she knew, had hoped Cherry had started to see the foolishness of the worry.

"Sadie, I'm fifty eight." The words, the tone, the glimpse behind the familiar blue eyes, hooded with age and here so unguardedly desperate, made Sadie's heart leap to her throat. How much it had taken for Cherry to come clean, to admit to this and ask for help. This was dear, sweet, tortured Cherry, the sometimes life of the party, the friend who'd shared nearly a lifetime of history with her, a little girl of sorts who needed her. The actual thought of Cherry being right, of losing her, was too much to bear or, at the moment, add to this situation. Sadie searched in vain for the right thing to say.

Cherry relieved her. "It's just so hard, impossible, for you guys to know what it's like. I've tried, believe me, to shake the feeling off, I really have. I hate it! I just can't help it. It's like… just something I can't ignore. It makes too much sense, and I know that's hard to get but it's like it keeps telling me to be ready, you know? Now my doctor thinks I'll probably need dialysis soon. I just wish…"

The dialysis wasn't new in Cherry's hypochondriac complaints, although the actual imminence of it was, but right now the overall picture needed addressing. "Honey, it's okay. I know, I really do. And I hate it too, we all do, that's why we've been trying to help you brush it off." Tears that had been welling rolled down her cheeks. "We didn't mean to make light of it, we just couldn't stand the thought."

Cherry, her own tears coming in release at this first real exchange, reached her hand to hold Sadie's. When the warmth, the connection, brought the outpouring to near embarrassment at the table, Cherry pulled her usual cover.

"I'm not dead yet. Let's not have the burial here."

The smile from Sadie, then the slight but unshakable laugh, gave way to rational thoughts.

"Alright, miss smarty," she said, loving the lighter look now on Cherry's face. "We need to get this stuff figured out for you." This wasn't the time to try any dissuading on the death idea. That would definitely, however, seriously need to be addressed later. "First, I completely disagree that you owe him for the expenses. If you feel like you have to clear your conscience, then tell him that part. I don't think you need to, but it doesn't sound like he's in any position to do anything about it, so if you have to do it to feel okay with it, then do it. Then…"

"That's easy to say."

Sadie relented with a pat to her hand. "I know. It sure is. But let's just go from there. The most important thing is, you have to make sure nothing about what you did can be considered directly illegal. I mean, it sounds like some could have been, but you have to cover yourself so he can't report it."

"That's part of why I'm getting so scared. One of the agents seems to be asking too many questions lately, about his pay and stuff, how Glenn does things. I mean, I've wanted to put it all back anyway, but now this guy has me freaked on top of that. It may be nothing, but still."

That little detail sent a shiver through Sadie. She couldn't let on to Cherry. "Well, let's get practical now. Do you have any idea what that figure would be? Without the paycheck stuff."

"It's a lot. Eleven. Thousand"

Sadie did her best to not look astonished. "Then, that's what we're dealing with. Do you care if I talk to Cat? I really think we need another brain in this, make sure it gets done right."

"I suppose so. But just Cat, okay? I mean, I know I did this and all, but it's still super embarrassing."

"Okay. It's just that I don't have any idea how to fix this. We need to make sure you don't get in trouble."

"You can't believe how this feels. Carrying it all alone…"

"You don't have to. Not any more. What about Jeff? Does he know?"

"Oh, good grief, no. He'd probably turn me in."

"He would not."

"Well, maybe not. But one thing I thought of is, if I told him, maybe he'd be like an accomplice or something."

"Hey, that's what I am right now."

"Oh! I'm so sorry! I didn't mean for that…"

"I know. I was joking. I'm not worried about it. Besides, if I thought you'd been an out and out crook, even though you're my friend, I wouldn't help. But you're not, and you have to know that.

Believe that. Jeff knows you too. And I think you owe it to him to fess up. Tell him you hadn't wanted to make him a part of it. He loves you. You need him to talk to, to help you through this. And we will get through it. We will."

"I just don't know if I can, but I'll think about it. Listen, promise me you won't say anything to the others? Except Cat? It's just so humiliating. I hate that I even am dragging you and her into it. I was so sure none of this was ever going to matter, then it did and it got too late, and I just don't know what else to do."

"I promise. And, if it helps, I'm honored you told me. I really am. Cat will feel the same way. Don't ever feel bad about that. We know you by now, remember?"

"And therein lies my worry," Cherry grinned.

The moment eased, the lunch was finished. All the way home Sadie's racing mind tried to settle on the ramifications of the whole thing, including for the role she'd just accepted. What Cherry had done was pure embezzlement. Poor Cherry. Stupid Cherry. Why in the world had she done that? Excuses were never the bottom line reason, but Cherry hadn't even offered one. The important thing for now was getting her out of it, but that accomplice thing was really no joke. Sadie debated involving Cat, but quickly rethought and couldn't wait to get home to do so. She needed help in this. Cherry needed it. They had to rally, there just wasn't a choice.

"She what?!" It was the response Sadie had expected from Cat. "Was she fucking nuts?"

"You should have seen her, Cat. She's really scared. She never meant for it to come to this, that's for sure."

"Shit. This is what she was leading up to during a little talk we had at the last reunion. I never pushed. Damn."

"That's how scared she is. It just broke my heart."

"Should we just give her the money? I can. I'm not loaded, but I can. Could she just put it back without getting caught? I'm not even sure that's the way to go, are you?"

"I have no idea. We've got to do this right, though. However we do it. Wish we had Syd's input, but Cherry swore me to secrecy, except to tell you."

"Hey, she forgot to swear me in. I'll call you right back."

Sydney was as stunned as Cat, and in turn called Maggie for her advice from the perspective of manager of the restaurant's books.

Maggie knew the workings but not the legalities, which Wren would probably know. By the end of the night, Wren had called Sadie for more information.

They all had immediate and wrenching concerns, not the least of which was the embezzling, but too, the apparently heightened and self imposed death sentence Cherry was putting more stock in than any of them had thought. Especially Cat, coming from the belief it could manifest by sheer will if Cherry didn't direct it otherwise.

"Maybe going to jail would give her a jolt, make her want to stay alive till she got out," Cat said to Sydney midway through the talk.

"You don't mean that."

"No, but damn. She's got to get a grip. She could really just up and die if she keeps this up and believes it."

"Cat, a person can't do that. She's not any closer to it than we are. Just wait till she's eighty and laughs at being so silly. Cher's just a worrier, that's all. She's been that way for as long as we've known her. You know that."

"Yeah, but still, she's messin' with danger thinking like she is."

"Let's figure out her real danger for now. She actually could be in trouble with this, Cat. Shocks the hell out of me. Cherry, of all people. I'll go in with you on the cash, by the way."

"Thanks, we can talk about that later. I'm not sure she shouldn't turn to Jeff. For a lot of reasons. Knowing him, he's been socking away for retirement since college. We need to think about it. Just glad to have a backup head. She can't go this alone, neither can I."

Wren was putting the primary focus on making sure Cherry avoided any legal issues. If she wasn't their precious Cherry, the choice to withhold help would be easy. She'd broken the law. But, the fact she was already paying it back aside, a criminal she was not. Punishment could come in many forms and Cherry was the most likely of all to render her own brand of justice. She'd already done so through regret and anxiety stemming from the act, rather than getting caught. That was enough for them. They knew they were setting their own standards. So be it.

"It sounds like she's going to have to give it to him and hope he's just glad to have it back," Wren said, calling Sadie. "If she tries to cook the books, she'll implicate herself. Tell her that's the one thing not to do. She needs to hold something over his head, some ammunition and it sounds like she has some, so he should, if he's smart, accept it and let it go at that. Tell her Cat said to call her, and to not doing anything until then. And I think she needs to know we're all in on it, that we're in her corner. Blame it on Cat, she can take it. How are you with all this?"

"I'm just so sad for her, can't think of any better word than sad. You should have seen her face when she was talking. I don't know which is worse really, the money thing or her being so afraid of dying. Her spark is gone, that old feistiness. She did crack one pretty good joke at herself, that was the only time I saw any of it. I can handle this, it's fine, just so you all keep in touch and let me know where to go from here."

So continued the cycle of calls, calls safer than e-mails and the best way to get the others' immediate takes. The rally to aid one of their own was personal, each slant personal, together creating a whole picture. Sydney was the most practical, Wren not far behind, Cat and her esoteric thinking, for once, agreeable but putting this in encompassing terms that included more. Sadie was the mainstay, seeing each angle as valid, especially Maggie's, who pushed Wren's view of telling Cherry they all knew and were behind her. In the end, Cat was elected to render the verdict, one that would hopefully extricate Cherry from this and from all of her haunts.

Chapter 7

Cherry hadn't gone into depth with Sadie about the doctor's concern, aware her ongoing complaints were often boring. The money issue was enough, one thing at a time. She also hadn't been entirely sure of anything until the latest appointment. His suspicion was confirmed. There was no more debate or hope of hedging the inevitable. She'd have to start dialysis soon.

She hadn't talked to Jeff yet even though she'd promised Cat last week she would. She'd decided the necessity of doing so hinged on the results of this appointment. If she didn't need dialysis, if she didn't have to miss work, maybe be replaced, the fear of getting the money put back would not have been so immediate. The snoopy new agent and his wife had just had dinner at Glenn's, diminishing the intensity of that threat for now. Repayment had to be done soon anyway because of her life's limit, but telling Jeff could be stalled just a little longer until she had time to gather more nerve. She'd used the last of all she had in the telling to Sadie.

He sat reading the newspaper after supper, his ritual to unwind from the day. It'd been a rather rough one but standard. The school board, he'd ranted all through the meal, was looking at cutting the music program, which didn't affect him directly but he would regret its demise for the students. Cherry cleared supper dishes. She could wait for later when they'd have their evening ice cream. Or she could do it now.

"Honey, I need to talk to you for a minute," she said, taking a place in her nearby rocker. This was even harder than talking to Sadie, although it shouldn't have been for any reason Cherry could imagine. Jeff was Jeff. It felt strange to care so much what he thought, callousness having set into the marriage early, but watching his eyes look upward as he put down the paper, she realized how much she did.

"I went to the doctor today. I didn't tell you at supper because it's really bad news. He said my creatinine numbers rose again. He said I'm finally going to need dialysis for sure. Before summer."

Jeff's eyebrows burrowed in the painful knowledge, sympathy and concern bathing his face. He reached over and patted her arm.

"Well, we've known that could be the case. It'll be fine, honey. I'll be with you all the way." He spoke softly, with the best words he knew to comfort. "Did he say anything more about a transplant? Does he know where you are on the list?"

"All he said was what he did when he signed me up. It's usually about a five year wait. He'd hoped I'd be able to make it that long, but guess that's not going to happen now."

"We need to talk more about asking the kids. Or Mark. They really deserve to make up their own minds. I know they'd want to be given the chance to at least be tested."

"No. I said it before. I won't do that to them. It's like asking them to risk their own lives. Or even having to make the choice and tell me no. I won't."

Jeff shook his head. "You're not being fair, honey. You're really not. I'm sure each one of them would jump at the chance. There's no real risk, you know that. I wouldn't ask that of them either if that was the case. They're going to feel awfully bad we aren't considering their feelings in this."

What he didn't understand, because she'd never expounded, was how ultimately futile a transplant was in light of her destined end. She couldn't ask anyone, especially her children, to give up a vital part of themselves just to ease her limited remaining time.

"I'll think about it, but right now there's something else."

She started with her fear of missing work due to the dialysis routines, and finally into the connected urgency of fixing something she had done. It'd been for them, for their budget, she hoped he saw it'd been for him and the family, to help make things better, not that he wasn't providing just fine, it was simply for the extras in life that make living enjoyable. She spewed out the story, rambling nonstop to get through, the words garbled and interrupted by tears but coming nonetheless. He patiently and silently heard her out, unable to speak if he'd been given the chance.

"So," she concluded, making the finish seem like a redeeming factor. "Cat said they're all going together and can come up with six thousand to help out, so that only leaves five thousand we have to cover. I know it will put a dent in your 401K but..."

"Cat? Your friends know about this?"

"I sure didn't want them to. I was hoping to tell just Cat, she's the one who spread it to the others, looking for them to chip in. I'm not happy about that either."

"Cherry! This is a felony! I don't care so much about why you told them as how much you can trust them not to turn you in! I mean, maybe one of their husbands or somebody..."

"They're not like that, you know them. They would never! And they wouldn't let anything slip either! Come on, let's just figure out what we're going to do."

Jeff was by far in too shocked a state to think rationally about details right then. He leaned back in his chair and closed his eyes. Cherry was not sure at all of what he thought, what he'd say next, and suddenly, if he'd go along with the plan. His hair, it'd thinned over the years without her noticing. The light of the reading lamp shone through to his scalp. Gray was giving him a rather distinguished look, again unnoticed as the years had fled so otherwise preoccupied. What had she done to him, her prince of sorts?

Why had she never seen how much she loved him? The feeling now wasn't of a flash thrill, it was deeper, and it hurt. Like a million times worse than throwing out favorite old shoes. How much he'd suffered with her and for her, not just health issues but with Jenny. He'd loved her parents so much, for her. And she'd just done this to him.

She knew why the girls had forced her into this, they'd told her, but their reasoning just hadn't held water. She was to share with Jeff, Jeff was her husband. He deserved to know, and she deserved to have him lighten her load. Secrets fester and create problems on problems. They were forcing it because they love her and respect her marriage. Those were their words exactly.

She knew that'd been mostly Cat's doing, it smacked of Cat's philosophies. Cat, who'd told the others. In her humiliation, she wasn't all the way fond of any of them right now, a defense against their knowing this part of her life, but also for going along and insisting she confess to Jeff. She alone, though, had put herself in the position of needing help. Cat would say that was perfect. She'd done it to have this outcome and finally be free of at least this secret. Cherry supposed the point was to finally tell Jenny about her father too. They should all know by now that was not going to happen and should just let it be with that same respect. That would be real friendship.

"Honey, we'll get through this," Jeff said, his eyes still closed in thought. "One thing at a time."

"Jeff, I..."

He interrupted her and leaned forward, reaching over to her with his hand. "It's all going to be okay."

They talked until bedtime, forgoing the ice cream that night. He objected to the girls chipping in cash, he could do this himself with his pension, until Cherry explained the girl's rationale. If any suspicion was ever cast, the lump sum shouldn't be traceable back to one source. He relented, but told her to assure them they'd get it back. He'd take care of his part the following week; she should let the girls know. The sooner this was over, given the other concern, the sooner they could get Cherry mended.

His arms wrapped around her as they fell off to sleep, a comfort she hadn't realized she'd missed as the years had interpreted it as unwanted foreplay. His warmth, his unfailing love was bringing hers out in reciprocating tenfold. Maybe the girls had been right. Hopefully that applied to their theory on Glenn.

Glenn hadn't aged well, neither had she, and his slime factor had gradually chiseled away all but a hint of his sex appeal. What replaced it was a bond of partnership, some in crime no less, but a bond. She wasn't a contributor to what he was doing, she'd told herself that all along. She hadn't been the one who swindled innocent victims. No one but Glenn had been injured by her part in skimming from his ill-gotten gains, yet the injury she'd done to her soul, husband, and friends made her feel no better than him.

The partnership, however, along with the ever present remainder of appeal, had created for her a quasi marriage. He had filled the gap over the years of her yearning for something more. He made it exciting, or at least bearable, to come into work. He was someone to dress for, put care into make-up for, an unattainable goal to keep reaching for. His occasional overt niceties fueled her secret fantasy, despite her miscuing their message. Even – especially – in some releasing way, his dark side lent to the chase. He was a bad boy, a forbidden and despicably bad boy, the kind who was tantalizing against better judgment. The thought of him whisking her off to bed made for dreams that sustained her through the humdrum of life.

She'd never thought anything juicy would happen, she wouldn't know what to do if it went that far. But his place in her flights of fancy had become real and necessary. It wasn't clear if it could be called love. Infatuation maybe, she thought. Lust. What was important, and what she knew for sure, was how much it mattered what he thought of her.

She'd gone over all the ways this confrontation could be bypassed, but Wren was right, there was only one. If she deposited the money, split equally among the accounts, there would be no way to explain those sums if need be. If she adjusted the books by backtracking, that could be caught in an audit. There just was no other way.

In light of the fact she didn't have the money to repay anything but the dummies, she opted to mentally and physically dismiss the rest. Sadie was right. Reimbursing the expenses wasn't necessary. No need to even mention that. Taking them had, after all, been legitimate in essence, and since Glenn had never stopped her, he must have considered them alright. She did her best to push away all thoughts of those, and concentrated on how to ease the rest to him.

He didn't acknowledge her as she entered his office, other than by a raised hand to wait. Cherry took a seat. The brown paper bag, looking much like her lunch, fell to its side at her feet. She quickly straightened it.

"Yeah?" Glenn finally said.

"I need to tell you I'm finally going to need dialysis, not yet but coming up, and I'll need some mornings off."

He briefly looked up. "Sorry to hear that. You've been dreading that, right?"

"Thanks. Yes, I have. It's been a terrible thought. I'll make up the time evenings or take work with me if that's okay." She paused as he nodded, then came out with the rest. "There's something else that I feel terrible about. And I'm sorrier than you'll ever know. I've been taking more money than I should."

That got his full attention.

"Go on."

Cherry couldn't look him in the eye. This was it. It was time. Her heart pounded in her throat. She bent to pick up the bag and stood, placing it on his desk. "I owe you this. From bits here and there out of the trust accounts. I'm paying you back all of it."

He stared at her as his hand tilted the bag for a look inside.

Cherry had to keep talking or faint. "Eleven thousand. Cash. I'm sorry. It was just that I needed it at the time. I'm sorry. I didn't take it out of the real accounts, just the fake ones. I…"

Glenn didn't hear the rest. In addition to the shock of it all, for the first time in eighteen years, his trusted bookkeeper, a friend of sorts and working companion, had just called him and the agency unethical.

"I'd understand if you hate me, but…"

"Cherry." He held his hand up to stop, sitting back as he did so to think. "Until I figure out what to do, I want you to leave. Stay home. I'll let you know."

Cherry, shocked, started to defend herself but his hand rose again. She shut his office door behind her. Through watery eyes, she took in as a whole what had been her home away from home for so long. The familiarity of the walls, the cheap reproductions hanging on them of flowers, one of a barn. The cheesy picture of Glenn with the mayor. Her desk, the computer, the ownership of her little corner of the world. The smell in the air, the stacks and files of stale, aged paper. The stench of parts unholy.

The side drawer of her desk squeaked its customary rub as she opened it to retrieve her purse. Maybe for the last time. The pictures of the kids, grandkids, the family one and three tiny stuffed animals rested against book-ended manuals. They needed to stay. Glenn needed to see she wasn't gone forever. She found her way to the hall and reached for her coat on its hook next to

Glenn's. He hadn't asked for her key. That was good.

His expected call didn't come the next day. The agony of the hours alone with her thoughts drove Cherry nearly insane. She'd considered the varied reactions of his, even the one he had given but, even in that worst case scenario, it hadn't felt like this. He'd left her with a feeling of such wrongdoing, of such a personal criminal mind, this reality had none of the redeeming qualities supposed to be attached to the outcome.

None of it made any sense. He couldn't seriously do anything drastic; he couldn't risk what she knew of his operation. He certainly couldn't report her, even fire her. He probably just needed time to put all this into perspective. Every time a thought like that calmed her, a frightening one replaced it. He could fire her. He could send her to jail. He wouldn't do either, but he could. She pushed away images of herself in a trial and the creeping one of life in a cell. It took every ounce of strength she had, and went against her worrying nature, but to give in was worse than to fight them.

The feeling of relief of having cleared her conscience just wasn't coming, as much as that'd been her purpose. Her anxious uncertainty of what Glenn would do overpowered any sense of accomplishment. This waiting maybe was her punishment, and rightfully so if it was. There should be punishment involved. She'd squared herself with life's unfairness and had taken it more than a few steps too far. Not far enough for severe retaliation, still dread of what lie ahead fought to overtake her. Glenn wasn't done. He would make sure she did her due suffering.

She desperately regretted calling the accounts fake, that very likely had pushed him unnecessarily. But Wren had insisted she find a way to let him know she knew. Leverage, Wren had said. Make sure he knows you have leverage against him. When it just slipped out like it did, at first it felt good to have found a way. Then panic, especially at his reaction. It was done; there was no changing it now. Cat would say it'd been the perfect unfolding of her intent. Cat was full of shit.

Jeff wasn't faring much better than Cherry, although keeping himself together was needed. He said he believed her, and was heartsick she had worked for so long under such conditions, but couldn't tell her he didn't entirely buy Glenn's crooked ways. Jeff, honest to his core, couldn't fathom how someone in that business could have sustained as long as Glenn had if much of it was true. And if nothing substantial could be held over his head, Glenn was in a position to prosecute her. They'd face that when and if the time came, but for now, he had to wait as she did.

Glenn didn't call until a full week had passed. He asked that she come in the following Tuesday at one thirty. The suspense was nearly over but his tone and instructions had not brought relief. How odd to pick a Tuesday. What a strange time of day. If he had said Monday morning at eight, the implication would have been of a talk before starting a normal work week. Tuesday at one thirty didn't say that.

Neither did the shiny new front door knob or the box on her desk in the familiar but strange feeling office. The head of a stuffed animal peered over the box's edge. Cherry's racing heart sank. Then, as she looked up at Glenn's open door and saw two other people, it seemed to completely stop.

"Come in," Glenn said, pointing to a chair. "You remember Diane and Ben?"

Cherry nodded and forced a half smile. The accountants.

Glenn took charge of the talk. "Okay. Just to catch you up on the process, I gave Diane and Ben all the records to go over and make sure of their accuracy. Or lack of accuracy." He turned his attention to them. "And you've found all the discrepancies, right?"

They agreed.

"Cherry. I need to know why you ever thought some of the trust accounts were not legitimate. That really, really interests me."

Cherry's mouth was so dry her tongue could barely move. "It was just that... the names... your name on them... the cash part of deposits..."

Glenn shook his head in disbelief and disappointment.

"I'm sorry." She couldn't think of anything else to say.

"I imagine you are." Glenn had regained his initial composure. He folded his hands on his desk. "I don't know what has me more disturbed. The fact that you took it or that you thought I would operate that way."

Cherry was now out of words.

"This is all very hurtful for a lot of reasons. We've worked side by side for how many years? I liked you, I thought you liked me, or at least had respect for me as your boss. I can't tell you how this has caught me off guard. Really."

The room went completely silent, the accountants knowing their place, Cherry too.

"But, anyway." Glenn decided to get down to business. "There are a couple things working in your favor here. One, we found that you'd started repaying the accounts even before this lump sum, right?"

"Yes." She was stunned they'd been able to discover her untraceable method of not only out but in. With a fleeting shiver she also had to accept something else. The fake accounts were really real if the accountants knew and had gone over them with such a fine tooth comb.

"And paying it all back. That's in your favor too. I can't keep you on, Cherry, you understand that, I'm sure. But, between your efforts at making this right, and your health condition, I'm not going to press charges."

He looked at the accountants who again agreed, then squarely at Cherry. The ball was in her court. She tried to hold his gaze, to tell him everything with just a look, but had to stop. It wasn't working and was painful.

"Thank you." Hopefully that said it in part.

"So, that's it." He stood to dismiss her but stayed behind his desk. "Your things are on your desk."

Cherry took the cue and stood. Halfway out of the door, his voice stopped her.

"I wish you well, Cherry."

She turned, and with quivering lips that had held for as long as they could, she thanked him one more time.

Chapter 8

Jeff partially understood Cherry's depression, but the relief of not having legal charges filed made it hard to fully grasp. She could find another job down the road, and the following months off were actually good timing for planning the transplant to have her health issues solved. Dialysis would spread over time, another argument now against going that route. The logic seemed clear to him.

For Cherry, logic was the furthest thing from her mind. Nothing about logic was valid. She'd used her best logic all those years working for Glenn and had misjudged him so very terribly. How could that have happened? Was she that dumb, that overtly and wrongly suspicious of everything, that she had imagined all she saw? Apparently. There really was no denying that. It brought into question all she knew and spun her head in circles.

The emptiness of long days alone in the house was agonizing. Every glance at the clock brought a memory of where she should be at that time. Eight fifteen. She should be starting the daily filing of yesterday's claims. Ten o'clock was break. Eleven forty five always held anticipation of what she was having for lunch. Twelve fifty five should have been the scramble to get back to her desk. Five o'clock was quitting time with a check-in to Glenn and a wish for a nice evening.

She missed him. She missed the way he used to smile into her eyes when she'd land a good joke on him. She missed the familiar feeling of family there. His presence united them. She was his special confidant after the guys had left for the day. They had been a team. For eighteen years, they had been almost married in a way. They hadn't ended right. They had just stopped. No one just stops, there's always some closure, and the lack of any was a black hole. She fought to fill it but nothing could do that except closure itself. She needed him to know how much he had meant to her. She needed his forgiveness. Neither had any means of happening.

As a consolation, she told herself the ending was his fault. He wasn't supposed to fire her. That just had not been necessary. She really hadn't done anything so awfully wrong. Getting fired had been a factor of the risk, but why hadn't it seemed more likely? And why hadn't she thought of the rest that was happening, not just about him but everything? How would she begin to pay back the girls without her old steady job? How had she planned to do it anyway in the time she had left on this earth? Why hadn't she thought that far ahead? All she had done was trade one debt for another. Jeff would take care of the payback; he'd already said he planned to despite her objections. But it wasn't his to do. She supposed, in the whole scope of things, maybe it was, since he'd benefited from the ill-gotten gains all along, but that probably was rationalizing. Or was it? She had no idea anymore of what was true or not.

She had told the girls and Jeff about the firing, leaving out the accountants and fact Glenn had obviously been aboveboard all along. Sticking to the original story allowed her to keep her only remaining shred of dignity. Part of the truth had accidentally come out during lunch soon after with Sadie, but Cherry had quickly retracted and connived a covered up version. As much as she loved and trusted Sadie, love and trust were now shaded and at a premium. She had to reserve some for herself.

To others, including the kids, she said she'd quit to take care of her health and asked Jeff to back her. The lie made it easier to stay in the house and avoid situations where the topic might surface. Weeks of being a hermit fit her mood and yet contributed to its ongoing intensity. She had nothing to do but think.

What a horrible thing to have happen toward the end of what was otherwise a good life. She had been good, she'd tried her best. Being good had always been forefront. Even taking the money had good intent behind it. She'd just been trying to set things right.

Sadie had even said that once. Sadie knew her intentions had not been bad. It just wasn't fair, but then, wasn't that the story of her life?

The denial, the anger, brewing inside her served only to heighten her underlying despair, and no one around her was helping. Jeff, having just come to her rescue, had been gaining in his role as protector, but his assertiveness was diminishing her new warm fuzzy feelings toward him. He was already on to the next step in their lives, a future, one that included a transplant over dialysis. They argued, he lost, but she could tell that he had no intention of dropping it.

The girls had been amazing but their support, too, seemed to hit a flat note. They were lovingly clear they didn't want her or Jeff to pay back the money; they had given it to help with no expectations of having it returned. They were proud of her for facing Glenn and thrilled the worst outcome had been the firing. She should take it easy, enjoy her time off, begin to think ahead. They bypassed in depth the idea of impending death with expressed hope that was no longer an issue. After all, she'd cleared her conscience; she'd probably been letting guilt build all these years which made a happy and long life seem not deserved. That now was groundless, wasn't it?

They always did that. Dismissed her fear. Sadie said it was because they so hated the idea of losing her. Cherry felt they just didn't care. Granted, they'd helped her out of the mess with the money, and had always included her in the reunions and called now and then in between, but when it came to believing her about dying, they didn't seem to want to be burdened. Of course it was a downer and unpleasant and sad, but it wasn't trivial. Not to her. They should have understood.

She had no idea they did.

"We need to leave her alone for awhile," Sadie said in a call to Cat. "She's dealing with this like she needs to. She's pissed. At the world. If she wasn't, I'd be more worried. I just wish she'd let me in to that head of hers, you know, let me know why she's thinking this, but she's not up to it yet."

"I know, I've tried too. I just wish she'd put all that anger into telling whatever reasons she has just to go to hell. She can't keep thinking they're true, that much I know. Even Syd agrees. Kind of.

She's open to any way to get Cherry back on track."

"Hopefully once she comes to terms with this other, she will be."

"You know, I get how it's awful to be fired and all, but geez, she just got a free get-out-of-jail card. What's the huge dilemma? Is she that embarrassed or what?"

"From the things she's said before, I gather she thought her boss liked her more than that, that he…"

"Had the hots?"

"Well, she kind of did for him. Just the way she talked. I know she'd never do anything about it, but I think she was hoping he at least looked at her as a friend more than an employee, like a work family thing. I'm not sure how she thought that would matter with something like this, but apparently she did."

"Been there. So okay, how long should I lay low? You know I'm not good at this. Just sitting back."

"The last time I called there I got Jeff, and I asked him to keep in touch with us too, when she wasn't around, just so we'd have his take on how she's doing. I'll let you know."

It didn't take Jeff long to call, and for more than an update. He needed their help; he wasn't making headway alone, and asked Sadie to recruit the others. Despite his qualms of them knowing of her embezzling, not only was he sure they'd rise to this occasion, he knew they could reach her in ways he just couldn't. He'd witnessed the way they'd operated from the beginning. These women, maybe all women, had a language all their own.

Cherry seemed to be retreating day by day into a private void, functioning but missing luster. Her initial anger, much of which he suspected had been directed at herself, had been better than this. He was at a loss for how to help her. Part was surely the upcoming dialysis which would make anyone nervous, and not feeling good wasn't helping. Migraines were sending her to bed at least twice a week. His attempts at talking seemed to heighten her withdrawal, so he relented and left her alone. His worry grew, his hands felt tied, his tested love for her never wavering.

The only concrete thing he could do, and he knew it was against her wishes, was to quietly delve into the issue of a transplant just to see where options stood. He suspected she was simply afraid of the operation itself, so if he could round up information, along with a donor, it might be the answer to ending all this. Her excuse about a donor's health just didn't hold enough water. People donated everyday with no repercussions he'd ever heard. Her fear was the operation. It had to be.

In enlisting the girls help, he filled in Sadie on what all was involved. She called the others to explain. Cherry was blood type O, but even another O would need to have antibodies that matched. The blood type was just a place to start. Jeff was talking to the kids as well, and odds were one would be a fit, but if not, would they do it? Would they just be tested? And by the way, of course Cherry didn't know, so mum on this part of activities.

Of the five of them, Sydney and Wren were Os and both jumped at the chance to save Cherry. Why hadn't Cherry ever said very much about her diabetes leading to this? She'd always had complaints over the years of one malady or another. This was big. She, for once, should have said more. How interesting. How unlike Cherry.

"So this dialysis thing, it'd be just a temporary fix?" Sydney asked Wren on the phone. "She'd need a transplant sooner or later anyway?"

"She's apparently headed toward complete kidney failure, so it sounds like yes. Dialysis means going in about three times a week, take hours, probably isn't much fun. Plus for her, it just means putting off the inevitable."

"Yuck. Hey, she has insurance, doesn't she? Could she keep it even after…"

"She never had it there, stayed under Jeff's family policy. Guess her job's co-pay was too expensive. Sadie already asked."

"Unbelievable. At an insurance company! But whew, good as it turned out. So anyway, if Cherry's so hell bent against this transplant idea, what if she gets pissed and won't talk to us?" Sydney asked Wren on the phone. "She could, you know. I can just see it."

"I don't think so. I think she feels like she owes us, so she'll be decent. To our faces."

Sydney laughed. "Have you met Cherry?"

"I know, but I think she's really scared, Syd."

"You think she thinks the operation would kill her?"

"Either that or that it won't. I think she's given up, she really thinks she's due to die and shouldn't mess with it. With nature or God or whatever. I'm betting that explains her secrecy."

"Geez. Really?"

"Afraid so. Years ago I remember something coming up about it, from her diabetes, and she got really quiet, let it drop. I can imagine any other reason she'd do that."

Sydney sadly agreed. "I bet you're right. I feel for her, I really do, but I just don't get it. She's such a fighter, about everything else anyway, why isn't she fighting this?"

"She may be. We just don't know."

"This whole embezzling thing might have worn her down. You think?"

"Seems like the timing is kind of hand in hand. So, Syd, are you going to be tested?"

"That's actually why I called. Yes, are you?"

"Sure."

"I said that at first too, and I am," Sydney said. "The more I think about it, though, it's kind of scary."

"Me too. I mean, I'm going to, and if I match I'll do it, but it feels different than I thought it would. I didn't think I'd think twice but I did."

"I'm glad I'm not the only one. It's just that the reality of living with only one kidney is something I've never had to think about."

"We shouldn't feel bad. We're just thinking it through, that's all."

"Dan says I'm not being silly or selfish, it's a big decision. He says I should do whatever I want. Big help."

"We still don't know if either of our antibodies matches."

"What if we both match? We draw straws?"

"Let's just take this one step at a time."

That's exactly what they did. They scheduled their tests with the results to be sent to Cherry's lab per Jeff's instructions. The wait worked to settle their minds. It was a big decision, but this was Cherry. There really was no debate.

Jeff called Sadie to say he'd talked with all three of the kids, he hadn't mentioned the deal with the stealing, something the girls should be aware of in case it should slip, but as far as the transplant and all it entailed, they were completely for it. Steve, the oldest, wasn't a match; they already knew he had Jeff's type B. He would be, though, a big help in talking to his mother and convincing her. Bruce was going to be tested for antibodies, and the best news was Jenny. She'd be tested too, and was so filled with excitement at hopefully doing this, it was going to warm Cherry's heart. There were a few fences there to be bended, if the girls didn't already know.

Jeff, finding strength and sensible momentum when needed, said he was also contacting Cherry's brother Mark, unsure of his blood type but recruiting him for any help he could give. Cherry respected Mark's opinion, although she'd never admit it. Cherry was certainly a pistol, wasn't she, Jeff laughed. He was sure the girls saw beneath her sometimes annoying little antics, her recent big one notwithstanding. Please pass along his thanks again for that. He appreciated their caring and coming to her aid, now and always. They were probably often closer to her than he was.

If any of them thought Cherry would be happy about having forces reined in around her, they would have been wrong, but none of them did. They knew she wouldn't just lie down and take it. Jeff, the safest and most at hand, got the brunt of her dismay.

"Call the kids back," she said in no uncertain terms. "You called them, you call the back. I'm not having a one of them go through that for me."

"Nope. Won't do it. You don't want them to help, you tell them."

"Jeff! You had no right. Do it. Now."

"Actually, I'm sure they'll be calling you. When they do, it's up to you."

He had decided enough was enough. Besides the overriding benefit of having the disease finally mended, the logic of her being free to move forward and find a new career to erase memory of the last one had propelled him to take a firm stand. He hadn't expected her to be so ardently against it, and for the life of him didn't know why she was, but if she couldn't see clearly the options before her, he'd step up to use common sense.

The calls came quickly. Steve was so sorry he wasn't a match; he would have gladly been a donor. His daughter was a possible match but still under the age of consent, not a viable option according to what he'd read on the internet. The internet had great information, he said. Had she taken a look? Cherry was floored at the extent of not only his knowledge but concern. Still, this shouldn't involve him. This was a private matter, just between her and God. Rightly or wrongly, the family's assumed say-so was infringing and boxing her into a corner.

Bruce, who was submitting to the test the following Tuesday, at first fought her flimsy reasons against him doing so. She politely assured him she knew exactly what she was doing. He didn't buy it, and fully intended to keep his appointment, but cajoled her for the time by dropping argument, experience saying it'd be for naught.

Mark didn't give up so politely. "That's bullshit, sis. You're just being stubborn. When the hell are you going to outgrow that?"

"I'm not being stubborn, just practical. You're not a match anyway, are you?"

"You bet I am. I don't know about being a complete match yet, we'll see, but so far, so good. Be honest. Why aren't you all excited about us wanting to do this?"

"Because. It's complicated."

"I'm listening."

"I just won't, I can't, ask anyone to give up a kidney when who knows if it will work or..."

"Or what?"

"Nothing. It's just risky."

"Jeff home?"

"Yeah, why?"

Mark knew his sister well. He dropped the topic and made excuses. He'd call her back when she was alone and as this thing progressed. Who or what she was protecting, he didn't know, but he did know there was more she wasn't saying. She was all he had left of the family; her wellbeing mattered regardless and was a responsibility he was not going to shirk. They had found a new bond of sorts after losing both parents, though old differences still stood between them. Those weren't so strong anymore, maybe never really had been, they'd just been a set-up by parents who knew no other way. If he was rotten and Cherry was good, the lines of discipline were easy. Those inflicted characteristics had made them become who they were. They'd both suffered, mainly Cherry. She so deserved to live now.

Of the calls that meant well, the one from Jenny rocked

Cherry's world.

"Mom, I'm doing it. I'm at least getting tested. And if I'm a match you're not saying no. I won't let you go through dialysis."

"I really appreciate it, Jen, I do. But no. I'm not letting you do that for me, I…"

"If you don't, I'll never speak to you again."

"Why would you say something like that?"

"Because I mean it. Put Dad on."

Cherry handed the phone to Jeff. Jenny, the only person she had thought wouldn't care one way or the other, had just changed the landscape of her plans. She could call Jenny's bluff, she could push, but her knowledge of her daughter left no doubt a fight would be useless. She watched Jeff's face as he talked and listened, saw his nods and heard his agreement. It wasn't over, Jenny may not match, but a sinking feeling told Cherry to brace. Her personal objective had just met with an unmovable brick wall.

She went to bed without speaking to Jeff, not having clear thoughts to say. Fleeting visions of this actually happening sped too quickly to fully imagine. This was still her life, her choice. Jenny couldn't possibly withhold all communication. Forever. Until forever came. How horrible to spend her remaining time in exile from the one relationship she'd worked so hard to maintain. And what about Daisy? Would she be gone too? How unfair to be pinned between two choices when neither was what she wanted. Maybe this was part of her punishment. If so, it rightly felt like hell.

By morning, she'd regained some stamina, stamina without answers, just fight. She'd call Jenny later, talk sensibly to her and explain the best she could that this decision was hers alone. Jenny would bend. She'd have to.

Jenny didn't.

"I meant what I said, Mother. Now, let's wait for the results. If I'm not a match, if Uncle Mark isn't, or your friends, then…"

"My friends?"

"Yeah, didn't you know that? Dad said a couple of your girlfriends are the same blood type and volunteered to be matched too. I'm doing it, though. They're just in case I don't match."

Cherry had to say goodbye before she said something to regret. Boiling anger over such perceived deceit and blatant disregard of her wishes by everyone supposedly loving her blocked any useful thoughts from forming. She paced the room, unable to sit, unable to know what to do. If they really loved her, if they cared at all, they'd respect the decisions she made without question. That certainly wasn't asking too much. She'd made mistakes, but that was human. She didn't deserve to be treated as such a subhuman person. She was almost sure of that.

Anger kept at bay any self pity she felt but couldn't hold it completely for long. When two bowls of ice cream turned self pity to self loathing, she bowed her head in prayer and tears, begging for help to find the strength to resolve this and all of her problems. Not trusting anyone, and no longer herself, it was the only place of refuge to go.

Cherry, for better or worse, was starting to come unraveled.

Chapter 9

Mark came up from the city that Saturday for a heart to heart brunch with his sister. She really didn't feel like it, but a good meal was something Cherry rarely refused. He picked the restaurant, the best in town, and suggested it be private. No offense to Jeff.

"This is nice, Mark. Really nice. I mean, having lunch with you, and this place. We only come here on our anniversary."

"You deserve something nice more often than that. How are things with ol' Jeffy?"

"Good. He's been great. I haven't been the easiest person to live with lately."

"Lately?" Mark couldn't help himself, but did it with a grin.

Cherry just smirked and looked at the menu. They placed their orders before getting into the real reason for the lunch, which Cherry guessed was a variety of several. That was fine. She had an agenda of her own.

"You know," she started. "We don't have to pick at each other. We're all grown up now. You weren't the easiest person to live with either."

"Hey, my thoughts exactly. I apologize. I was trying to be funny. That's actually part of the reason I wanted to do this which, by the way, we should do more often. We're all that's left of the family, I guess that's part of it, but it just seems silly not to be more in touch anyway. For one, I think we're a lot more alike than all that silly ol' kids' stuff."

A slew of Cherry's old outward resentments of Mark's free

spirit melted away at his comment. "Thanks. I'd like that. I think we are too. I always wished I had more of your... I don't know, your 'what the hell' attitude, I guess."

Mark gave a robust laugh, not caring what tables looked. "This is so great! Really, you did? I always wanted to have your conviction for things. Not that you were always right, but at least you stuck to your guns. I was all over the place. Didn't know what I wanted. How cool is this? I love it!"

Cherry beamed and took a bite of her salad. "Would be nice if Mom and Dad could see us."

"Yeah, well, they'd find fault somehow. They'd probably say we should have brought the grandkids or something." He stopped at the look on her face. "Well, they would have."

"They're gone, though. And they tried. They did their best."

"I'll give them that. But I have to tell you, I think their best was seriously lacking. I don't know which one was worse, her for being so narrow minded or him for going along with it. They did a number on us, Cher. They really did."

Why his words now carried so much weight, she didn't know. He'd talked like this for years, disrespectful, before and even after their deaths. But the caring Cherry had lately for anything people related had waned too much to argue it.

"Remember how she could zing with one of her little comments?" Mark was saying. "She could make you feel wrong before you ever did anything."

"Yeah, but Mark, the stuff you did..."

"What a game. A stupid one, but fun. Just to get a rise out of them."

"It all was a game?"

"No, not all. I suppose not much of it really. Just my nature, I guess. But they certainly egged me on. Indirectly. I remember I used to ask Dad first if I could do something, he'd say yes, she'd say no, so no it was. He'd never, ever, stand up to her. Pissed me off."

In a flash, Cherry saw shades of her and Jeff in the marriage of her parents that would appear bad to Mark if Mark knew. It had always been such a good feeling to have emulated them, to carry on their traditional ways but, if Mark really had a point and he apparently was sure he did, both sets may have meant well but erred just a bit.

Mark wasn't done. "I think what they didn't do was actually worse. They didn't even love us just because we were their children. We had to earn it. I think that's why I pulled all the shit I did. Testing, you know."

"You did a lot of testing. That's what I remember." Cherry wasn't ready to give up her noble image of her parents that easily, not to mention hers with Jeff. "But I don't know how you can say that. They loved us more than anything. We were their life."

"I sure as hell never felt it. Not the real thing anyway. But yeah, I gave them a run, didn't I?" Mark started to chuckle but stopped. The memories weren't that fond. "I always had the feeling you'd have liked to kick it out once in a while too. Underneath your little good girl façade."

"Oh, I'm not all that good, trust me," Cherry said, looking down at her plate. It was interesting, this honesty, but she knew her limits. "I guess maybe there were a few times. It's hard having a conscience sometimes. You certainly had more fun, that much I know."

"Remember that time we were supposed to go to the library but we met up with Terry and Ronnie who had money and we all went to the fair? You had a blast!"

"But then I told on you, said you made me."

Mark let it go. "There were some good times, that's for sure."

"Sorry for telling."

"No problem. You were just being who they wanted you to be. They had us pegged. Labels. They just labeled us."

"They weren't bad, Mark. Quit talking like they were the devil incarnate."

"Hey, I loved them too. And am grateful, really. It helped me think for myself. I'm just trying to be a better parent than them. That's the way it's supposed to work. Learn from their mistakes. You. You've been a better mother than she was, I bet."

"I highly doubt it."

"Oh, come on. She was a piece of work."

That touched a nerve. "Why, Mark? Why in the world would you say something like that? That's terrible!"

"Sorry! I know you two got along, but…"

"Yes, we did. And I miss her. A lot."

The sentiment didn't surprise him much, although the emphatic way she apparently felt seemed overblown at this stage, after all these years. But as their entrées arrived, Mark turned the talk to the main reason for this get-together. Cherry's impending transplant.

"It's all Jeff's doing. I've told him all along being on the wait list is all I want. I can do dialysis until my time comes." She inadvertently meant that in more ways than one.

"But if one of us is a match, you wouldn't have to wait. He's just thinking of you, Cher, wanting you to have this over. Is it his pushing that's making you upset?"

"I'm not upset, I'm… I just don't want to put anyone through that, it's chancy, you know."

"Why chancy?"

"Asking someone to live with just one kidney."

"Lots of people do. It's no big deal. Hell, I'm willing. Ready and rarin'. I'm set up for the blood work on Monday."

"Mark…"

"Oh say, did I tell you I got a call the other day out of the blue from Joe Hennigan, remember him? Looking for a job. I put in a good word for him with HR. Poor guy. Sounds like things are a mess. Just got divorced."

"From Kathy Goodman? Or was he on his second?"

"Her, I assume. Said he got married way too young."

"They dated all through high school, but were always breaking up and getting back together. Too bad."

Mark grinned. "You must have caught him on the rebound then, in between?"

"What are you talking about?"

Her startled look deserved a full blown laugh. "Under the bleachers, after a football game? Your little make out session? Whew! Steamy! Could hardly watch for more than like five minutes until I saw it was you!"

"It was not! I was just…"

"I loved it! Good little bad Cherry, having some fun. Loved it."

Cherry had to smile; there was no other defense at hand. It felt kind of good, briefly, to be united in mischief with him. Then it turned disconcerting. The idea of ever doing that didn't fit her image of herself back then. Funny how memories faded so quickly. Or become twisted into ones you want.

They reminisced about old friends, family life, neighbors, and who was where now and what were they doing. The mellowness of Mark, his matured sense of things, with its still skewed but content vision of how life worked made him seem the older of them. He had grown, she had not, or it seemed so in her mind. She shook off the feeling. It couldn't be right. She'd been through so much more than he had, and if not, she'd at least internalized hers and learned. Guys just didn't do that. They grew, but unaware. Still, fun as this was, and such a needed deterrent, that unsettling aspect persisted.

"You keep in touch with Cindy?" Mark was asking. "How's she doing?"

"I actually haven't talked to her in years. She's in Wyoming, married with two kids. Happy, I guess. We do Christmas cards. That's it. Don't have much in common."

"I get those too. Knew about her kids. You'd think she'd want to be closer. We're pretty much her whole family now too. Suppose she has her dad's side, though."

"I don't know think she's ever come back to visit her mother's grave. That's kind of weird. But it's her choice, I suppose."

"Some people aren't into that. It's just an empty dead body to them."

"Even so, it seemed like I took Aunt Marcia's death harder than she did."

"I doubt that. She flew back and forth for months when Marcia first got sick. She was probably halfway prepared. That part was different with our mom. A big difference too, wouldn't you say?"

Cherry didn't have an answer. Mark's waiting look made her come up with one.

"They both were way too young," she said with downcast eyes.

"Well, yeah, but…" And then, having grown up with his sister and the way her mind worked, he had a thought. "You're not thinking just because they…"

"Who knows, Mark."

He was dumbfounded. He hadn't seriously meant it; the words had just left his mouth. The notion fit her, sort of, while being completely ridiculous. He probably needed to tread very carefully.

"If you're worried, don't you think this transplant is the answer? I mean, it looks to me like it's a clear way out of…"

"I'm not worried."

"The hell you're not."

"Stop it. I know it's silly. I really am not all that worked up about it. Really. It just was a thought that crossed my mind. That's all."

"Does Jeff know you've been having these thoughts?"

"There's nothing for him to know, Mark. I told you, it's just something that dawned on me, for a minute, naturally it did, so don't look at me like I'm nuts. But I don't believe it. And I'm not worried."

"And," he gingerly leaned in on his elbows, "you're a lying sack of shit."

Cherry could confess or stick to her guns. He didn't seem to be judging the situation, but then again, this was Mark. The old Mark still resided somewhere under the classy sport jacket, a jacket paired with a black t-shirt that had a tie printed on it. Mark hadn't changed all that much.

That may not be a bad thing.

"What if I am? What if I'm scared to death? Literally. There's nothing I can do about it. Nothing."

He sensed, beneath the finality portrayed, she was asking him to come to her rescue. None of his well earned areas of expertise could be called on to be of much help. He'd have to wing it and hope he'd come up the right thing. It'd be nice if he could just hug her and have that convey what he meant. Or shake her until this idiotic notion fell out of her head and hit the ground smashing into a thousand pieces. The image of that loomed as his words took shape.

"Boy, I guess I would think that too if I was you. The logic of it, I mean. I'm so sorry for you. For me. I can't stand the thought of losing you."

"That's why I can't talk to Jeff about it either."

"Of course not. I get that now. The only thing is, when you said there's nothing that can be done, I really think there is. It seems to me that the transplant, and everyone running to donate for you, is a sign. Look at it as though you've been given a second chance. And take it. Stare this thing in the face. I've seen you knock a bully on his ass. I know you can do it."

She had to smile, but was in no way able to concede that easily. "But what if that's not the answer? I could die on the table, you

95

know. Or, what if I don't, and I'm going against nature? I just don't think I should be interfering. That's the feeling I have."

"That's the bottom line, huh? Well, let me think. I see what you mean, but okay, number one. If you think this is preordained, and you die on the table, then you've done your part, right? You've helped it come true." As ludicrous as it sounded to him, he had to play into her train of thought.

Cherry had never considered that angle. It didn't, though, fit completely. "But what if I live through it and come out fine, and shouldn't?"

"Then I'll rent a bus and come run you down."

He kept making her smile when she didn't want to. "Mark, I'm serious."

"Me too. Boy Scout honor."

"You got kicked out of Boy Scouts, remember?" She watched his smile flash and fade in wait again. He was pushing her to commit or continue. "I'll think about it. I will. It's just that it's so complicated, I don't know. I'm not making any promises."

"Deal. Meanwhile, I'll see if I'm a match. If I am, it's yours. Do with it what you want. Throw it in the garbage…"

"Jenny is insisting too."

"Look at it this way. Maybe nobody matches, then you won't have to make a decision on even doing it. I say relax, just see what happens."

She seemed to agree. They finished with dessert and a drink at the bar before splitting to go their own ways, Mark satisfied he'd done what he could but unsure if it'd made a dent. He knew his sister well. She wasn't good at bending once she had her mind set on something, and this fear of hers seemed too deeply seeded to be obliterated with just a few words. What a number their parents had done. Even in death, they were still managing to ruin their child's life. He hoped with everything in him it wasn't too late for Cherry to see that. This wasn't about dying or following God's will, this was about living in the shadow of fear and all its supposed glories. What bullshit. It was going to take more than today to change a lifetime of thinking, if that was even possible.

He wondered why so much had rolled off his back and she had absorbed it at face value. They both were fighters, that's for sure, at least their parents had given them that. It was just in such opposition directions. She fought to uphold, he fought to upend. Crazy. Over the years, he'd been so sure she'd wised up and put her spunk to much better use. It had seemed like it from all he knew. She had so much to offer, could be a kick and a half, was one of the savviest people he'd ever met. Gullible, but never in a million years would he have thought she'd be this gullible. This verged on complete irrationality. The transplant had to fix it. He or someone would be a match and there'd be no way for her to refuse. That would end her nightmare.

Cherry hadn't appreciated his take on their parents; he had overstepped his usually ranting. At least he hadn't brought up the suicide this time, although there wasn't much left to say. Neither of them had understood it, yet at the same time they fully had. Their father's quiet unhappiness had been such a part of his life that his death of choice seemed somehow both a shock and very fitting. They eventually just left it alone.

She had to admit Mark had a point, not about their parents but the transplant. Maybe being so cornered into it was a sign in itself. Her destiny could be to die on the table. That possibly was her intended means. Except then someone, likely her Jenny, would be minus one kidney for no reason at all. It'd just be thrown away, unless it could immediately go to a more worthy recipient, someone on the wait list. Maybe that was the round-about way for this to work out in some unknown grand scheme of things.

She stopped herself. All of those ideas meant she'd be dead. For as many years as she'd carried the knowledge, at this moment it felt imminently real. A cold shiver ran down her spine. All of the redeeming justifications for going ahead with the surgery were suddenly shaded in black. This really was a death and life matter, not just for her but Jenny, or someone dear, or a stranger. The decision was way too big. Something like that bus Mark joked about would be an answer and take the deciding out of her hands.

She looked both ways as she crossed the street to her car and headed home, foregoing a planned stop at the convenience store to replenish her supply of snacks.

Chapter 10

On the cusp of Mark's brunch came a call from Cat, not good timing for Cherry when she was off balance. Cat was the one person she needed her full wits in a row in order to do usual combat. She also hadn't spoken to any of the girls since learning they'd been in on the transplant matching. Cat apparently had no idea what she was risking in calling.

"Hey, Cher. Whatcha doin'?"

"Who's getting matched, Cat? Why?"

Cat hadn't expected that right out of the shoot. She'd planned to tell her, although probably later, but Cherry had just set a new tone to the call. Or not, Cat though quickly. Let's just jump to the heart of things if that's how it's going to be.

"To answer your first question, it's Sydney and Wren. They're the only ones with your blood type, otherwise we all would. About the why? I'm not even going to honor that. They, we, love you."

"Love isn't going behind my back and doing exactly the opposite of what I want!"

"Well, not to argue, but sometimes it is. Or seems right at least. The motive is pure love, trust me. Now, why are you so against this transplant?"

"Because I am."

"That's a piss poor reason. You can do better than that."

"Probably I could. I just can't think right now. I just had a whole go-round with Mark. I'm not in the mood to talk anymore."

"Good ol' Marky! How is he, anyway? Remember when he'd

come down to Highland to see us? You, I mean? We took him out with us to Jimmy's. He was a hoot. Not sure he was even legal then, but whatever. Remember he had a thing for Wren? That was cute."

"Yeah, well, who didn't."

"You?!"

"Cat. No. Of course not. I meant all the guys."

"I kinda did for a while. Then she became more of a sister so that shot that." Cat was hoping a touch of shocking honesty might be the key about now.

"You did not."

"Oh yeah. Everybody has secrets and we all think they're more terrible than the next guy's. There's mine. No big whoop."

"Did you ever…"

"Sure. Had to experiment. Not with Wren, though. I swear. For one, she was too bony. You were much more my type. Perfect love handles."

"Geez!" The flashing mental image repulsed her, despite the warm rush of being chosen, and chosen for one her flaws.

"It's true. I'm not sure why love should have such boundaries, you know? I don't."

Despite the fact she was sure Cat was lying, Cherry fought back welling tears. Was she really so desperate to be loved that Cat's comment had nearly put her over the edge? It just had been an emotional day. That was all.

So much for jumping right in, Cat thought. What a sidetrack. It was okay, Cherry probably needed it. Still, there was business to get to; this wasn't just an ordinary call.

"Back to Mark. What'd he have to say about all this? Does he know the whole thing?"

"What whole thing?"

"About you're premonition of going early like your mother did."

"He's pushing the transplant, just like you guys."

This was like pulling teeth. "And you don't want it because, if you've got such a short time left, why have anyone do that?"

"Yeah."

"See, that's that big heart of yours. I think it's a horseshit reason in the scope of things, but it's coming from a good place, I'll grant you that. The only thing is, wouldn't God want you to feel the same way about yourself? I mean really, since everyone is created equal…"

"Don't talk religion to me. You know you don't believe it."

"Oh yes I do. This part anyway. I totally believe we are made in the image of God and it's our duty to honor that. Big time."

"What's that got to do with anything?"

"Everything. You know that story about the guy asking God to save him from a flood, and pretty soon a boat comes along but the guy says no, he's waiting for God to do it? Or something like that. I think God is sending you the transplant idea, and all of us chipping in, to save you from an optional destiny, so that it doesn't happen. That's the way it works, seriously."

"You don't know that."

"I'm just saying, think about it. What if I'm right?"

Cherry was finally up to fighting. "What if you're not? What if I have it done, take someone's kidney, then up and die. Right on the table. What then? Is that God's plan too? Leave someone with only one for no reason at all? Who knows if the doctor could get it to someone else in time or if…"

Cat decided to keep pushing. In her world, that's how things got done. "First of all, it's no big deal to only have one. That's all anybody needs. Besides, what you just said about someone else. It's the same thing as the boat. Only you're the boat. Someone else needs one or somebody else needs to give one, and it's not even your business to know why. That's the way it works."

"Oh really? What if I make it through and live for like a year. Tell me that's not a waste for somebody else."

"Could you be any more… Sorry. I'm really trying to help here. I highly doubt God…"

"I don't mean to be rude, Cat. You and the others just saved my ass with the money thing. But do not, do not, talk God to me. You don't get it. Nobody does."

"You think God wants you to up and die?" Cat put a bit of emphasis on that, hoping continual pushing was the way to reach her.

"No but… Yes."

"Why? Why does that make sense?"

"I wouldn't have the feeling so strong if it wasn't true!"

Now was the time to bring out the big guns. "Listen, please, sweetie. I know it's real. It has to be almost unbearable. But it may not mean what you think it does. What if it means a death of part of yourself? Like the stealing part. That part of you died. It's over and done and out of you. It's dead! It's not a part of you anymore. All you have to do is see that and the feeling will go away. That really could be it. I think it is. Doesn't that make a lot of sense?"

"None at all."

"It certainly does to me. I get chills just thinking about it. Good chills."

"It's ridiculous."

This was a bit exasperating. The theory was as plain as day to Cat. How to put it to Cherry so it did to her too was the problem. She had to try, she owed it to Cherry to do her best and had vowed before calling to not rest until done.

"No, not really. Like divorce, that's a death of a marriage…"

"I'm going to divorce you in a minute here."

Cat laughed. "Okay. Suppose it's too much to ask just to think about it? Anyway, how's Mark? Did he ask about me?" Humor was right up there with honesty.

Cherry relented. "He was too busy bashing our parents."

"Really? Why?"

"He thinks they ruined us."

"I used to blame my mother too. What a shame parents are such easy targets."

"I know. It's especially bad when they're gone and can't defend themselves."

"But it seems like most kids go through that. Didn't you ever?"

"No."

"I suppose with them being gone, the memories are different. I'd be pissed at that, though. Leaving you, especially your mom in her prime. Pisses me off for you."

"How could I? It wasn't her fault!"

That had gotten a bit of a rise. "It still happened, though. So, what was Mark's beef against them? I'm just curious. Nosy."

"Nothing worth repeating. I'm not going to talk bad about them. They didn't deserve it."

Dead end again. It was okay, all that Cherry wasn't saying was filling in the blanks, even though it was indicating a more and more fruitless chase.

"Maybe he's just mad his stuff with them never got resolved. Didn't have enough time. I'd have been a mess if my mother died that young. Not to mention furious."

"I was."

"Then, honey, don't do that to Jenny. The boys."

"It's not me! It's not on purpose!"

"It is if you don't do what you can to stop it."

The line went dead on Cat's end. Cherry had been pushed far enough. Hopefully not too far. Cat remained still, cradling the phone, hating for things to be left at this but deciding it was best not to call back today. She'd said what she'd planned to say, had gotten in all good points, and now it was up to Cherry. Cherry needed time to think. Cat needed, though, to talk, and dialed Sadie to fill her in on what had transpired.

Cherry barely heard Jeff's car pull in the driveway. Her thoughts were muddled, her heart racing, her bottled emotions too conflicted to name. Never before had she felt such fury. The thought of it being aimed at her mother's death came to mind and ruled momentarily as she fought it. It seemed wrong, so wrong, so undue such a good mother. Yet it was there and Cherry couldn't stop it. It was shaded with a matching fury at everyone now crowding in on her life, a fury, too, at life. She threw a book across the room, stood and threw another. She stormed out the front door with a slam as an unsuspecting Jeff came in from the back.

Cherry ran. She hadn't run in ages. It tired her quickly, it hurt her legs, she slowed some but kept going, too mad to cry or stop. The crisp air burned her cheeks and lungs. She rounded a corner and passed house after house, block after block. The normality of all the manicured yards seemed a blasphemous trick on the ignorant people inside of the supposed safety of homes. No one was spared, their time would come. The ugliness of living would catch up to them. Life was fair in that much. It played hideous games with everyone, some more than others but all would eventually be consumed. There was no out and if they thought so they'd be in for a shock when the insidious happened to them.

The waves of anger escaping from her with each pound of her foot to the pavement began to have faceless identities attached. She was livid her mother had died. Livid at herself for having needed her, for missing her. Livid at her own death sentence imposed by that relation. One by one, each wave flew back into her face, invaded her with unrelenting intensity, its wordless presence sharply stabbing over and over until she knew its name. All this time she had thought they were one but they weren't. It didn't matter yet right now it did.

Mark had started this, she was livid at him. He had no right to say what he had, to think that way about their parents. He was wrong. They had been the best they could be. Yes, their dad had always taken the sidelines but there was nothing bad about that. Their mother, maybe, had gone a little overboard with rules but only because she wanted them to always be at their best. She was good, she was, she was... no, she was good. She shouldn't have died, she didn't deserve it. The family didn't. Nobody deserves to have that happen.

Cherry blocked the hatred rising from an unknown region within her.

Images of Jenny and Stevie and Bruce as toddlers floated in front of her eyes. Her babies. She'd loved them so much, just like her mother had loved her. She hadn't needed to earn that. Her kids hadn't needed to earn hers. She could show it easier when they were good but even when they weren't, that didn't change her love. Every parent has moments of frustration. That doesn't mean they don't love them. Mark had been way off base.

Her and Mark's childhood mixed with her children's as her life rolled back like a movie. The picnics, the trikes and bikes, the bedtime rituals of baths and teeth brushing. Prayers on knees. Getting dressed for school mornings and extra special for Sunday church. Sunday dinners of chicken and mashed potatoes. Christmas tree decorating with tinsel and strung popcorn and homemade ornaments. Birthday parties and choice of supper on each one's special day. A good life for children. Good times. They didn't feel good now in review with their hinged melancholy, but they must have been at the time.

Cheerleading and Highland Street blurred into one. The girls. Classes. Jeff. Nick. The thrill of being in love. Or thinking so. Becoming a grown up, insecurity stripping its fun. Nick. Would he be told of her passing? Would he be so sad he'd feel bad he had never married her? Would he have chosen Jenny's name to have been something else?

Nick. Glenn. Her old job. Such a big part of her life. She'd been so wrong all those years, thinking what she had about Glenn. About the whole agency and the way it was run. She'd been wrong about every bit of it. How could that happen? What was the matter with her? Was she capable of making any kind of decision at all? Something about all that was not right. So much wasn't falling into any semblance of reality.

Nick. Glenn. The only times in her adult life she'd strayed from all she knew to be right had both ended in such deserved punishment. Was it enough? The moments of pleasure with Nick, the feelings he brought out in her, had resulted in a lifetime of payback. Jenny, so precious, was the jewel within all the trauma and lies, lies that never ceased to remind that transgressions don't go unpunished. She should have remembered that and not taken the money at work. She should have known better. All she'd ever experienced had told her that, why hadn't she paid attention? It was done, and she'd taken the repercussion. Hopefully it was enough so none was left to serve in the hereafter.

As exhaustion began to take a toll, Cat's call replayed in the present. Cat could tell Sydney, Sydney could call Nick. Sydney. Sydney was being matched to donate her kidney. What would it feel like to have Sydney's kidney inside her? To live for the rest of her life being so closely tied to her, someone she'd always looked up to? Or Wren's. Wren's was probably beautifully healthy. Mark's. Would his bring with it some of his wildness? A lack of conscience?

Jenny's. Someone she'd given life to wanted to give it back to her now. It wasn't supposed to work that way. How ironic to have half of Nick's heritage implanted in her too. What an unholy thought. Why was she thinking of him again? Was all this forecasting her final moments, this reliving of her life's pieces? She hadn't thought of Nick in a long time, other than today. Or was that part, and all that went with it, already gone and was Cat right, had she died without really dying?

Did she have to really die? But what if she lived and wasn't supposed to and then was damned to hell forever, just for another twenty or so years? Would God do that? Or was this transplant His lifeboat?

The thought of another twenty years was something she hadn't let enter her mind. Not having it made the thinking too painful. But could she? She looked up from the sidewalk to what was around her, all signs of things she'd known since birth. Did she really have to forego them, and all else that she knew? They were like her car's steering wheel so long ago after the horrible graveyard visit that'd started all this. So familiar. So life. She'd gripped it like she wanted to now embrace this sidewalk, this grass, these houses. Heaven was obviously unbelievably better but this, this, this was what she knew to be hers. How she wished she didn't have to leave.

Could the transplant possibly not be the life or death issue she thought? Maybe she could have just five years or so, enough to make amends and make it worthwhile and then succumb in some other way? The whole world, or this town, could go up in a bomb at any minute. Was she trying to take this into her own hands when that wasn't the question or answer at all? It was too big, too confusing, maybe on purpose. Maybe it wasn't hers to decide.

A neighborhood park brought a clearing with trees. She leaned against one and slid to its base with quiet sobs. She'd run and she'd thought and she'd released and decided as much and as far as she could.

Jeff found her huddled and cold and wiping her face with her shivering hand. He didn't ask. Now wasn't the time. He took off his jacket and wrapped her with it as he sat along side. Cherry buried her head in his shoulder.

"Tell the kids I'll do it," she said into the warmth. "I'll have the transplant."

Chapter 11

The question of who would donate began to override the one of doing it at all. The results of the matching ruled out Bruce and Wren, but confirmed Mark, Sydney and Jenny as viable. If the deck had felt stacked against her before, this decision for Cherry trumped it.

Her initial instinct was to go with Sydney, strong Sydney, who likely would be the least affected. She loved Sydney very much, and wished she wasn't an option, but of the three that were, Sydney had the least to lose if something went wrong down the road. Sydney didn't have children, none that could be counted as such. Her stepdaughter had a mother and didn't seem to be very dependent on Sydney for that kind of nurturing support. Sydney had enough money and knowledge to get all the help she would need if unfortunate circumstances happened.

But something about that didn't feel right, not withstanding the fact choosing anyone did. The more Cherry thought about it, her decision grew firm. She couldn't take Sydney's. She just couldn't. She already owed Sydney so much for being part of the bailout with Glenn, it was unfathomable to ask for anything more. Sydney had been such a good friend over so many years when it probably wasn't what Sydney would have chosen if she'd had choices. But she'd always been kind and understanding anyhow, especially when it came to Nick. That must have hurt Sydney even though she hadn't shown it. It wasn't fair to hurt her again. It was just too unthinkable to risk Sydney's life if one kidney was ever to fail. No,

Cherry couldn't.

The problem was, that same reason applied just as strongly to Mark. Mark had children and a wife on top of it who depended on him and loved him.

Jenny. Jenny was out of the question.

The doctor concurred about Sydney for a different reason. She'd be a workable alternative, but the odds of success tend to be somewhat better when a matched family member contributes, when that's an option and assuming a predisposition didn't exist of which both Mark or Jenny had been cleared. It was one thing to have the transplant, another to have it succeed, a detail at this point that was unsettling but no more so than everything connected with the whole issue. How much easier it'd be to just crawl into bed and pull up the covers and sleep until the end of her time.

Immediately after the results had come in, narrowing it to just the three, Jenny had called Jeff to reiterate her position. And then she called Mark and Sydney. This was her responsibility, her desire, so please, they didn't need to even consider it.

"Sweetie," said Sydney. "I understand. But your mother doesn't want you to. I'm sure she's told you that."

"Yeah, but you guys are good friends. She'll listen to you."

"I can try, but you know your mother. She'll listen to me about as much as she does to you. If that."

"But you'll talk to her?"

"The only thing is, she'll think I don't want to do it."

"That's okay."

"Not really. If she wants it to be me, I need her to know I'm ready and willing. Can I ask why it matters so much to you? All I know is her side."

"I just do. I want to. It's important to me."

"Why? Give me something to work with, Jen. I'd need to tell her something."

"That's all I've got. Please?"

Sydney laughed. "You're just as stubborn as your mom!" And in that same thought, somewhere off to the side, the relationship of mother and child brought to mind the eerie realization she was talking to her old boyfriend's daughter.

"That's probably the only thing I got from her," Jenny was saying. "And big boobs. Those I appreciate. So anyway, I really just called to give you a heads up that I'll be the donor, so you don't have to be sweatin' it."

The conversation ended with no promise from Sydney, just an offer for a kind ear if Jenny ever needed to talk. Besides loyalty to Cherry, Sydney had a personal motive in keeping her option open. She wanted to be the donor. The shift had started soon after getting the results.

"I think it's probably like finding out you're pregnant when you don't want to be," she confided to Sadie. "Your first response is, holy crap, which is pretty close to what I really did say, but then, like with the pregnant thing, the thought of an actual baby, a new life, hits you. So I want to do this. I want to help save Cher. It's really hard to explain, but it's like doing a good thing for somebody else would give me something I didn't know was missing."

Admirable as that was, it wasn't to be. When Cherry called, the letdown was even more than Sydney expected. She assured Cherry she'd still be willing if anything happened to change her mind, or if circumstances required it. That still was a possibility, depending on what Mark said, and with neither mentioning Jenny's name, the inference of that choice staying sour was clearly in the air.

Putting her personal wishes aside, Sydney had begun rooting for Jenny, although this was the wrong call to say so. She had to have Cherry firmly believe she herself was a steadfast backup. But Jenny had gotten to Sydney's heart. She didn't know why, Jenny was as closed as Cherry when it came to giving up glimpses of anything personal, still she couldn't dismiss the fact the girl was too adamantly on the offense to have it be anything trivial. Another call to Cherry, when the right words came to mind, might shed some light on reasons. On the other hand, knowing those two, Cherry was likely as clueless. A call though, would satisfy that withheld promise to do what she could for Jenny.

Mark wasn't as elated as Cherry had hoped to receive the news he'd been chosen. His wife, he said, had reservations, but not to worry, he was just fine with it. Sheila was just thinking of the kids and their future, but he'd assured her the chances of ever having the remaining one go bad were astronomical. He'd be honored to do it, and was glad Cherry had come around to having this done. Everybody was so happy for her.

Cherry had always found Sheila to be a bit of a control freak, a strange match for free spirited Mark, but had watched over the years as Mark settled down to become a responsible grown-up, probably thanks to Sheila. Sheila had never really taken to Cherry, things had been pleasant but surface, so that dislike could be playing into the matter too. Sheila wasn't family, not blood, she shouldn't have really a say. This should be strictly between brother and sister. Cherry knew as she thought it, it wasn't.

Then there was the wedding. Their middle daughter was getting married this summer. How long was the recovery, did Cherry know? He'd like to attend but this was important, so if he could do both, that'd be great. Cherry said she'd check and get back to him, but it was looking like her other options might be better. He didn't significantly argue.

That brought it back to Sydney who, in the meantime, had talked again to Jenny. Jenny's stubborn fortitude, even without stating yet any valid grounds, worked once more on Sydney. Whatever Jenny's reasons were, she was owning them. She was fighting, just like her mother, for what she thought to be true. That was a quality, along with the fortitude, that Sydney shared and held in highest regard. Those traits had joined her with Cherry, like Cat but differently, from the beginning. Sydney wondered if she'd ever told Cherry that.

"Of course I will," she told Cherry in the call about Mark. "I'd love to, I really, really would. And I will. I'm just wondering about Jenny. I know you don't want her to, I do, but you think that could be hurting her feelings? I mean, ..."

"I'd rather have her feelings hurt than have her do it. She's got to understand my feelings in this too. Is it that you don't want to now? I'd completely understand. I would. It's really huge."

"No, I have not changed my mind. In fact, it'd be an honor to do it. I'm serious. I'd love to. It's just that Jenny seems to want to so badly that I wondered if you'd explained it to her, told her your side so she…"

"You've talked to her?"

Sydney had to think. The last thing Cherry needed was to believe people were going behind her back. "I just wanted to know her reasons." There, that didn't give away Jenny.

"Why?"

"Because. From what you've said, she's got some really set ideas about this. I didn't want to step on her toes. If she wanted to that much, it would matter."

"You sound like you'd rather not do this."

"That's not what I'm saying. At all. I have to tell you, even the thought of it gives me a new sense of purpose. It…"

"This whole thing has turned into such a mess. Jeff shouldn't have even started it."

"You're not listening to me! I want to! I just don't want to come between a mother and daughter. Plain and simple."

"Like any of this is plain and simple."

Sydney was about at the end of her rope. It was so tempting to call her a pain in the ass but Cherry would likely take it too seriously. She softened the best she could. "I know this is hard. I can't even imagine. Just take it one step at a time. I'm here. I'm one hundred percent anxious to do this for you. But please talk to Jenny again first. Hear her out. Then let me know what you want to do. Like I said, I'm all set if you need me. And I'm not changing my mind. "Are we good?"

"We're good. I'm sorry. I'm just…"

"A pain in the ass. Quit worrying so much and just let us all help. We love you." That all had slipped out but felt alright.

She heard Cherry chuckle or hold back a cry, it was hard to tell which, probably both. They ended by talking about Sadie and Wren, since they had each spoken to them recently. How good to hear Cherry sound normal if just for a few minutes. This had to be rougher than anyone could possibly fathom, although Cherry, as usual, was unfortunately making it tenfold as hard. This wasn't really life or death, not in the grand scheme of things. How sad Cherry seemed to think so. Sadder yet, she wasn't open to seeing it differently.

Cherry wasn't sure she entirely believed Syd was feeling up to being her donor. The Jenny excuse was maybe a ruse. It was so hard to know just what to believe with everyone seeming to conspire against her. She knew they were all coming from a place of concern, and they weren't against her as much as deciding for her, but none of them had even half of the facts. It'd be so nice if they all trusted she knew what she was doing.

Except every time lately something went wrong, she questioned that herself. All the old doubts resurfaced along with new ones until Cherry couldn't even feel sure the sky was blue. They boggled her mind during the day and more so at night when sleep wouldn't come to relieve her. The qualms made no sense. She'd made the decision to have the transplant. Details should have fallen in place, not create more to muddle it. Things always had gone that way, though. There was always cause for worry of some kind. No reason this should be different.

Well-wishing calls came in from close neighbors, and the church circle put her on their prayer list. The teachers at Jeff's school sent home cookies and cakes, just why, she didn't know. She wasn't an invalid. Some stopped by too, with casseroles and stews, presumably thinking she needed her rest and shouldn't be on her feet cooking. The thoughtful gestures instead took away the need for the one activity that daily arrested her wandering mind. She had just developed a way to stretch thirty minutes of prepping a chicken dish into a good two hours when the invasion of food gifts began.

It was all very nice, though, if unnecessary, and rather an intrusion into her quiet. And there were those bothersome few who expressed surprise she wasn't more excited over the upcoming big event. What a beautiful thing to have so many donors. How loved she was and how lucky. She didn't want to discuss it; there wasn't much that could be said to strangers or even her friends. Jeff had obviously been giving glowing reports, so she covered and left it at that.

When the decision on a donor was settled, things would be easier to handle. The whole was still so overwhelming and seemed to have a will of its own, continually popping to the forefront of her thoughts, but she tried her best not to dwell on it. After this decision, the rest would be in God's hands. She'd prayed for help on that, had turned it over, and worrying would mean she didn't have faith in the answer chosen for her. She had to remember to hold tighter to its sustaining reassurance.

Then one day she was hit by the thought that maybe this decision should be included in the plea. Maybe all the confusion it seemed to be causing was to force her into giving up her input. The idea was the most comforting one she'd had in a while, and lulled her into a much needed nap after the prayer. She slept so deeply, the ring of the phone seemed part of a dream until she realized it was real.

"Grandma? It's Daisy."

"Hi dear. How are you? Is everything okay?"

"It's good. How're you doing?"

Cherry assured her she was just fine. They chatted a few minutes about Daisy's school work and tennis team and Grandpa before the talk took on a more serious tone.

"I'm actually calling, well, to say hi, and kind of to see if you would really think about my mom being your donor. She says she's going to be whether you like it or not, but that's not gonna work and she knows it. She needs you to want her to. Really bad."

"I know she'd like me to pick her. She's made that quite clear. It's just that I won't risk her health…"

"But you wouldn't be. That's the thing. We've gone on the internet, there's a whole bunch of information on it. You can look. She's talked to her doctor, too. It's not a problem at all. Tons of people do it and are just fine. She says that excuse sucks big time. That's why I thought I should call you. She thinks it's personal. Against her."

"How? Why in the world would I feel that way?"

"She just said the real reason is that you just don't want any part of her in you."

That took Cherry aback. "She's so silly. That's not true."

"She swears it is."

Cherry really had no doubt that was the irrefutable truth. Daisy and Jenny had always had a mother daughter bond as best friends, as had she and her own mother, so much alike and so different. These two actually talked.

"So, will you call her and tell her yes?" Daisy was saying. "It's really super important to her. She's been like a bat out of hell around here ever since this came up."

"Daisy Sun!"

"Sorry. She has, though. It's really complicated, it's all twisted for her, so please at least call her?"

"Of course. It's not like I never do. She can call me too. Should she know you've told me all this?"

"Sure, I don't care."

Of course not. She should have guessed. After assuring Daisy she'd think hard, Cherry changed clothes and headed for the library. A closer coffee shop had internet service, but the likes in there looked scary. She and Jeff should have probably bought a computer, but with both having one at work, that never had been necessary. She missed e-mailing with the girls, though. E-mails would have been nice through all this. Nicer than sometimes having to explain things in depth by phone.

The web had a wealth of information. She wasn't sure she could trust some of the sources, but the volume of legitimate sites confirmed without question Daisy's comments. Even so, something could happen. Why was Jenny putting her in such a position?

She waited that night until Jeff ran to the store, not wanting him to counter her side of the conversation. Jenny answered, and as usual got right to the point.

"So, are you going to take my kidney or what?"

"I went to the library today. I've been so worried it just wasn't smart, you know. I couldn't risk it being dangerous for you. You know I've just been thinking of you, don't you?"

"You found out it wouldn't, right?"

"Well, yes and no. It doesn't sound like there'd be much of a chance, but it still makes me nervous. I just don't know, Jenny. It's not that I wouldn't love having yours…"

"Then do it. Take it."

"But…"

"I was right. You just don't want mine."

"I do! I mean… Why is this so important to you? Tell me that. Be fair."

"Because. I need you to want it. To want mine. I just do."

"And I want you to always be safe and healthy."

"Just because you have diabetes and all this stuff doesn't mean I will too. My doctor said."

"But you don't know what will happen down the road. Anything could happen. A car accident could hurt your good one, a fall, there's never any guarantee. I care too much about you to take any chances."

"Then show me. That's my reason."

"What? I'm not following."

"Doing this. It'd mean you love me."

"You're being ridiculous, Jen. Of course I do, I..."

"Then let me show you I love you!"

Whoa. Cherry was silent, and in the quiet heard Jenny fighting back uncontrollable sobs. An urge to deny was her first response, but something deep inside told her stop. This deserved, required, demanded even, her respect. The other way around would have been easier to refute, she could have listed the ways she'd shown Jenny love. There were times of kissing skinned knees and sleeping aside her in the middle of nights to sooth away bad dreams and monsters. There'd been so much love, love had been natural. Some things might not have seemed like love, but as a mother now Jenny had to see they all were. Love had abounded, Cherry was sure.

She could tell her about the very beginning and its anguish, how love had made her carry through and bring her up with Jeff as her father the very best way she knew to do. Did she really owe it to Jenny to tell her? Everyone else seemed to think so. Was that at the bottom of Jenny feeling so lost and unwanted? It couldn't be. There'd been no difference in the way she'd been raised than the boys, and they seemed to have turned out just fine. No, telling didn't matter and wouldn't help. Not after all this time. Not when it could backfire so easily and not with other things at stake.

Jenny's love for her, thought, didn't belong in a category Cherry could do anything to change. All she could do was refuse to believe her, to challenge its validity with so-called proof. That wasn't what Jenny needed. Jenny had apparently made up her mind this transplant would answer everything. Yet allowing it went completely against her better judgment, and she was the mother, after all, the wiser of the two due to life's experiences and longevity. She had every right to go with her gut instinct on this.

Tough love had always worked before; this might be the time for its ultimate use.

It also might be the end of their relationship. Jenny might misinterpret it. She apparently had done so all of her life.

"Honey, I don't know why you feel that way, but obviously you do. I'm sorry."

"Then let me do this. Please."

Giving in riled every bone in Cherry's body. Why were things turning out like this? The situation with Sydney had turned to less than perfect, choosing Mark wasn't any better. But the fact it left Jenny as the most logical one seemed life's ultimate slap in the face. Jenny was an adult now, thinking for herself, no longer under her care and instruction but still her child. Her little Jenny.

This all was completely unjust. Unfair. Unholy.

Or not.

As disturbing and opposing thoughts jumbled around in her head, she breathed in deeply and heard herself answer. "If you're sure. Alright. Yes."

"You don't sound like you want to."

"Jenny! I'm still just worried about you, that's all. Other than that, I'd love for it to be you. Really. Now quit arguing before I change my mind. Obey your mother, for Pete's sake."

It probably wasn't the optimal way to seal such a deal, or for mother and daughter to bond, but Jenny knew better than to antagonize her by trying to go into more depth. That probably was all there was to it anyway, the fear for her long term safety. Her mother had never been one to go much below the surface. Doing this may not settle the question of how much love she had for her daughter, but, for Jenny, it would square the debt she owed her.

Cherry sat after the talk, trying to fully take it all in. She'd just committed to letting Jenny do this. That hadn't been the intent of the call. All she had wanted was to get a better of a sense of why Jenny was being so insistent. She'd found out, tenfold, which had surprised her into trying to fix it. Where Jenny ever got the idea they didn't love each other was beyond her. It was crazy. Poor Jenny. She should have said something sooner. It could have been explained pretty easily just in words without needing this. This was a grand gesture, too grand, and still didn't feel right, no matter what it accomplished.

Things had gone so fast, so against all of her wishes. She hadn't even wanted the transplant. Now the donor was the one person she'd expressly said absolutely not. It still wasn't done, she could take it back, cancel the whole ordeal. At the moment, that seemed the only way out, yet that would let everyone down and she'd have to explain and there weren't any reasons other than those she'd already stated, which should have been enough but weren't.

Why did they all say they were helping when what they were doing was making her feel small and insignificant? Was that love?

Jenny wasn't the only one feeling short changed. This was far, far worse. At least people listened when Jenny asked for something. Why didn't they do that for her? What had she ever done so terribly wrong to be left out in the cold at every turn? From the beginning, growing up, she'd been treated this way. Golden memories suddenly seemed jaded in light of what all this was bringing up and what Mark had said really was the case.

She hadn't felt any more loved than Jenny.

Cherry got up and went to the kitchen to heat up a leftover casserole. What was done was done. She was hungry.

Chapter 12

Jenny flew in ahead of the surgery to attend to last minute medical details and to spend time with her nervous mother. Cherry had been sounding edgy on the phone, resolute on the decision but not happy. Nerves were one thing, her attitude was something else. Their history of strife meant she likely wasn't the best one to fix it, if it was fixable at all. The effort, though, was one she had to make.

She had an agenda of her own mixed in with that concern. It had to be possible to have, or come close to, a mother daughter relationship like her own with Daisy. Why that mattered, she didn't know, her mother was no longer a vital part of her life. And yet she was. This was a piece missing, a goal left undone, a blank in her otherwise fulfilled world. Attempts over the years, as they'd led their own lives, had not done much to resolve it. They'd learned to simply work around their differences. For Jenny, that was not nearly enough.

This whole thing now could be an opportunity for change.

Both parents picked her up at the airport, and stayed close that day in family rehashing of events in their lives and the boys'. Steve was coming the day of the surgery; Bruce was unable but sent his best wishes. Jeff took the next morning off to drive both of them to the hospital in the city where the transplant was to be performed for an appointment to confirm final aspects. It wasn't until mid afternoon that Jenny was alone with her mother.

"This kitchen reminds me so much of Grandma's," Jenny said with a smile, helping Cherry put away the groceries they'd picked up on the way home. "Brings back lots of memories."

"You're memory is playing tricks. It's nothing like hers at all. Hers was all blue, blue little flowers on the wallpaper and curtains and tablecloth, little blue vases on the window sill. Blue, blue, blue. I don't have a spot of blue in here."

Jenny was shocked that the remark, aside from being obviously ludicrous, had an unmistakably bitter undertone against the venerated family matriarch. She looked around at the little orange flowers on the wallpaper and curtains and tablecloth, the little orange vases holding clashing purple African violets on the window sill over the sink. Nothing had changed since she was a little girl, and nothing, other than the color, was different than her grandma's. But her mother's slam of a cupboard door as the last of the food was shelved told her the topic was not up for discussion.

"Let's go for a walk, Mom. It's gorgeous outside."

"I'm a little tired from this morning. A nap sounds better to me. You sure can go, though. It is nice. Not too warm."

"No, I'll stay. Thought we could catch up some. Just us."

"Well, for a little bit. You want some of this cake?"

Jenny declined and plopped on the couch in the living room after pouring two coffees, waiting for Cherry to plate up a piece for herself. It took until its last crumb was gone for the talk to gain a nice momentum.

"So, are you scared?" Jenny asked.

"Of the operation? No. Not really. I think your dad is, probably more for you than me."

"He is not. He's really thrilled I'm doing this. He's been for it all along."

"He's always been a soft touch. Made me be the bad guy when it came to being practical."

Jenny didn't have much of an answer to that slant. She guessed it held a grain of truth.

"I'm sure that's why you often thought I didn't care," Cherry continued. "But it was because I did, you know."

"I didn't make it easy. I'm sorry about that. I really am."

Cherry reached for her coffee on the end table. "It's all water under the bridge."

"It's really not. I feel bad about it. I just didn't get, until trying to raise Daisy, how hard it is. To know what to do and all."

"Daisy is a fine young girl. You did a good job."

"I hope so. Thanks. Every time something came up, I'd wonder how you'd handle it if you were her mother, and…"

Cherry grinned. "You'd do the opposite?"

Jenny returned the smile. "It's just that it's hard. It's so much responsibility, being in charge of shaping a human life. A person. It overwhelmed me sometimes."

"My mother always said, 'Children are gifts from God.' She raised me and Mark, well, she tried to raise Mark, in respect of that. Sounds pretty much the same. That's good. I tried to do that too."

"Yeah." Jenny paused, not sure if treading on Grandma's name would contribute or end the conversation. "But from what I saw she was stricter than I am with Daisy. I kind of bend depending on the circumstances."

Cherry decided not to argue the point, despite feeling that was why children ran wild. Daisy had turned out okay, so to belabor it at this point was useless. "So, does Daisy know what she wants to do when she graduates?"

"She has no idea!" Jenny laughed, throwing up her arms. "Actually that's probably fine. I don't know how kids can be set on something at that age when they haven't tasted hardly any of the world yet. She'll figure it out. She's leaning toward graphic arts or photography. She'll land on something eventually."

"I suppose those are good ambitions, nice hobbies anyway, if nothing else."

"Oh, I don't know. I think she'd be able to earn a good living, maybe great living, at either. She's very creative."

"In my day…"

"In my day?!" Jenny got up for more coffee, tenderly swiping at her mother's knee. "You sound like you're a hundred!"

Cherry had to laugh. "Smarty pants. You know what I mean. Things were different. The choices for girls were between being a nurse or teacher, it seemed. Even then, it was just something to do until she got married."

"Daisy says she's waiting until she's thirty five to even think about getting married. Said just in time to still have kids, if she wants to by then. Right now she isn't sure."

"Can't you talk to her? I mean, it sounds like she has a bad idea of it or something."

"No, not her. She just has a lot she wants to do besides that. Travel, have her own place, find out what she wants and who she is, that kind of thing."

"Aren't you afraid you'll never have grandchildren?"

"If things keep up like they are, I'll be too busy anyway. It's fine. Her having kids isn't my decision."

"Well, no, but…"

Jenny changed the subject. "Your friends. They didn't all get married right away, did they? And Sydney. She became a designer, right? So even back then, it wasn't just black and white."

"No, but we were right on the edge of things starting to change. A lot of girls still did what their mothers did. It seems like that was about the time morals started going down too. In the sixties. Seems like it all went hand in hand."

"So," teased Jenny, leaning closer. "Did you have loose morals back then?"

"No, of course not. And it's not funny. Morals are still sliding. It's not a good sign."

Jenny let that go. This wasn't a topic she'd win. She was much more interested in opening her mother to real talk. "Did you ever date anyone but Dad back in school?"

Why in the world would she ask that? If she was just on a kick to share girl talk, that was one thing, but if she had suspicions, that was something else. Her demeanor, though, didn't seem to indicate any ulterior motive. Thankfully.

"I did in high school." Then Cherry did some skirting of her own to put an end to that subject. "I had my share of fun if that's what you're asking. Good, clean fun. Fun doesn't have to mean breaking all the rules."

"Like I did?"

"I didn't mean that. Besides, that was a long time ago."

Jenny needed to not brush this under the rug. "I know. But all I was doing when I did those things was trying to speak, you know? Trying to tell you what I wanted and needed. I wasn't trying to be a brat."

"It doesn't matter, I said. It's over. You're a fine young woman now. That's what counts."

"Do you get what I'm saying, though? I was just trying to have you let me be who I was, so I, I don't know, tried to make you listen, I guess. I need you to know that. It wasn't because I didn't love you."

So that's where Jenny got the idea she needed to make up for something. Cherry nodded, but took a moment to think. This was obviously important to Jenny. This, and the other half of the equation she'd alluded to so bluntly on the phone. The fact she hadn't felt loved in return. This was as good a time as any to set the record straight, although allowing her to be the transplant donor should have done that without all these words.

"I know you did, Jen. Mothers just know those things. You know Daisy loves you, right? You just know that."

"Yeah, but she and I've got a really different relationship. I just wanted to say it, that's all. Make sure you know that."

"Right back atcha."

Jenny smiled. Neither of them had ever directly said the phrase to each other in normal context, it just wasn't built into the way they communicated. How nice it would be to talk with her mother the way she could with Daisy, so easy, so open, so freely. Pushing would either bring it, a touch if nothing else, or make her mother so uncomfortable she'd get up for that nap. The importance of it was worth a try.

"I never was sure, you know," Jenny ventured. "That you loved me. I know it's probably silly, but sometimes I felt like I was just a burden. I'm sure I was, I…"

"Stop that. You know better. I wouldn't have gotten so upset with you those times if I didn't care so much. I don't know what you want me to say, or do. Nowadays you've got all the books and TV shows on self esteem and all that, telling you how to talk to your children, how to make sure everything you do is correct according to the experts. When I was raising you, even Dr. Spock was controversial. I know my mother thought he was hogwash. I had to figure things out all by myself, so mostly I did what my mother did. All anyone can do is to do what they think is right."

That was sobering.

"When I was a little girl, about five," Cherry continued, a sudden motherly need to teach and affirm her point seeming more important than keeping the private secrets of her past. "I almost drowned. I guess it took the firemen a while to get me breathing.

My parents were frantic. I know it seems strange to have memories from that age, especially being unconscious or whatever, but those moments are very clear, to this day. I remember hearing my dad begging me to wake up. When I opened my eyes I saw him, leaning between the firemen, close so I would hear him. My mother was standing right behind him, crying so hard. I'd never seen her cry before, not at all."

"You never told me any of this!"

"So I had to be put in the hospital to make sure I was okay, and my mother stayed until I could come home. She slept sitting up in a chair in my room. I remember that."

"Mom! I can't believe you never told me! Were you scared?"

"No, not with her there. I was too young to know it'd been such a close call. Kids don't know things like that. Then, when I came home, we were eating supper and they were arguing a little. They never did that. My dad just said he wouldn't, and he took Mark, Mark was just little, outside to play."

"I'm not following."

"My mother took me to her bedroom and sat on a chair, and made me stand in front of her. She told me I was never, ever, to go near the pond again. That I was a naughty girl for going there. And to help me remember to not ever do it again, she was going to spank me, and I shouldn't cry. I should take my punishment like a big girl so that I would remember. She got up to get her hairbrush. She spanked me so hard, on my bare bottom, I had to cry. It hurt so much. She kept spanking me harder and saying she wouldn't stop until I quit crying, and I wanted to stop but I couldn't. Then finally I must have been crying so hard I felt like I couldn't breathe, maybe I couldn't, that part I don't remember. Anyway, I never went near the pond again. I know that."

Jenny was speechless. Her heart felt as if it were actually breaking in two at the thought of her mother going through that. She couldn't yet fathom the mark it had left, just, for the moment, the pain.

Cherry straightened in her chair, uncomfortable at the memory but unaware of how it had sounded to Jenny. "So see, there're all kinds of ways to bring up children. To show love."

At that, Jenny began to sort out the whole. "But Mom, did you really think that was love? I mean, as a little girl? Did you feel loved?"

"That's not the point. That's what it was. She was trying to ensure my safety. That's love."

"But... I'm just saying... I think I'd have hated her. I do now."

Cherry started to stand. She was finished. "She loved me! That's what the story was about! I wouldn't have told you if I thought you wouldn't see that!"

Jenny had to think fast to get to the bottom of all that was being said. "Mom, come on. I'm just so mad that you, any child but especially you, was punished like that. I'm sorry. I don't hate her. I'm sure she was doing what she thought was the right thing."

"She was," Cherry said, settling back into the rocker. It may not have been a good idea to have told about the incident, but since it was done, it needed to be understood correctly. "You can't hate someone who did something out of love. You just can't."

Strange, stirred emotions were quieted at the sound of her own words. She'd never before spoken of that day. It had faded into the recesses of her mind the way it had been put in as a child. She had to cling to that interpretation. Jenny, no one, could disturb it. The disturbance already had come too close to making it into something it wasn't. Her mother had loved her. Her mother had simply rendered fair punishment. Her mother had kept her from ever venturing into danger again. That's what mother's do. Her mother had loved her. Amen.

"Did it ever happen again?" Jenny asked. "A... spanking... like that?"

"Heavens, no. She didn't need to. I was a good girl after that. I behaved, I never gave her reason to."

The look in Jenny's eyes, the doubt of such validity, raised again unwanted gut reactions. Cherry brushed them aside and fought for something to say to keep Jenny from voicing that look.

"I was good because I wanted to be good, that's all. It very likely made me who I am today. You can't fault something like that."

Oh, but Jenny could. "I'm sorry, but I think it was horrible. To make you afraid. I think that's what she did, I really do."

"Even if that's true, it still worked."

"So how come you never spanked us? You never laid a hand on any of us. Not once."

"There were times I thought I maybe should, but you're right, honey. I didn't. I couldn't."

"Why not?"

Cherry was not up for this. A tear snuck down her cheek. "The thing is, I took mine as love. I didn't want to chance that you or your brothers wouldn't."

"You didn't, even once, think maybe that wasn't love?"

"I suppose," Cherry breathed in, facing a hidden honesty for her daughter's sake. "Maybe deep down I wasn't sure. Maybe just like the doubts you've had with me."

In the briefest of seconds before Cherry averted her eyes, Jenny saw in their depths her real mother. The outward stoic strength she'd witnessed since childhood hid such vulnerability, such pain, such fear. She reached over and took her mother's hand in hers.

"I love you so much. I know Grandma did too."

"Of course," Cherry smiled, politely freeing the hold to stand. "Now. I'm ready for that nap. You still going for a walk?"

"Sure." Jenny stood too. That was as deep as things would go, but enough had been said to be an ending and new beginning. Then she remembered the afternoon's start and the reason she'd tried to initiate a talk. As much as the conversation had so unexpectedly covered, it hadn't answered what was bothering her mother. That ominous defeat she'd heard in her phone voice was again present like a hovering cloud.

"But first," she just had to ask. "And I'm not being nosy, I just want to help. Something's bothering you about this transplant. I can tell. It's not that it's me still, is it?"

Cherry stopped in the hallway. Her daughter's openness could be off putting, it certainly was something she'd never been taught. It also was occasionally, like this afternoon, quite heartwarming. Jenny deserved an answer.

But, how much of one. She looked at her daughter, healthy, shining with hope for the future, and instantly realized the generational truth stood to ruin her too. She was next in line. She had a right to be aware, yet what good had that done in her own life? It'd simply made the past years ones of worry and dark foreboding. Knowing couldn't change the outcome. Knowing had made no good difference at all.

"It's nothing. I was just set on the dialysis, you know. Hadn't planned on this. I've been praying for the right answer, am just not sure I'm doing it. My conscious tells me no, my faith says yes. I'm just feeling confused, but am going with yes."

Jenny walked closer with outstretched arms and embraced her mother, pouring every ounce of love and empathy she had in her into the hold. Cherry hugged back, smoothing her little girl's hair with a hand. There was no need for any more words. Jenny had to know she was loved. She'd never, ever been spanked.

Chapter 13

She made Jenny's favorite meal for supper, linguini with clam sauce, then begged out when Jeff and Jenny made plans to run errands and catch a movie. Surgery was only two days away, there was laundry to do and the house to tidy and Sadie was stopping by with a gift. Father and daughter could use some time alone anyway, she said, so they finally gave in and left.

Sadie came at seven as planned, with a huge box wrapped in pink, Cherry's favorite color, and tied with bright yellow ribbon. The girls had all chipped, she said. The content was for after surgery and wasn't much, but they wanted to her to recover in style. Under a pair of print silk pajamas was a plush, pale pink robe and slippers, and underneath another whole set in yellow.

"Oh my gosh! These are beautiful! And they cost a fortune, I'm sure," an elated Cherry exclaimed.

"The yellow's for Jenny. We weren't sure of her favorite color, but seems like everybody likes yellow, so we took a chance."

"It's perfect! You guys are so thoughtful! She'll love these! Me too. You know I do. Thanks so much."

Sadie helped her put the assortment back together, then followed her to the kitchen for coffee and a choice of three different pies. The talk stayed light, Cherry was in an extra good mood, and ended after not too long with a hug and teary well wishes. Sadie would come the morning of surgery, and if Cherry needed anything between now and then she should call. The others sent their same regards. They all were so happy for her.

"Would you do me a favor?" Cherry asked her at the door. "I've never brought up the thing abut me dying to Jenny, and I really don't want her to know. I wouldn't care except she doesn't need that hanging over her head. So she's not afraid. It just wouldn't do any good. I don't want her living with it like I have."

Sadie, not fond of lying or secrets, on this one wholeheartedly agreed.

Cherry rinsed their cups and plates, then gathered a laundry load. She debated on throwing in the new pajamas, washing publicly touched clothing always seemed the sanitary thing to do, but Jenny hadn't seen hers yet and they looked so nice in the box. She hesitated, but decided against spoiling the pretty surprise.

After changing into her old pajamas to include the clothes she had on in the load, she carried the basket to the top of the basement stairs. Years and years of routine practice allowed her to flip on the light with an elbow. That accomplished, she headed down the familiar flight.

It happened before she could brace. A loose sock, something, made her foot slide off the step. The basket flew as she fought to find something to grab. Every part of her body seemed to hit with each roll as she helplessly fell to the bottom.

The room spun when she opened her eyes to find herself flat on the cold cement floor. She stared at the ceiling as the seconds ticked and the basement finally came into focus. Slowly she lifted one hand, then the other, then shifted her feet to begin to stand. Nothing was apparently broken. She found the strength to get up, but each bend to pick up the scattered laundry was a strain. She took the items within site and loaded them into the washer. Good enough. She had to go up and lie down.

She was asleep in bed when Jeff and Jenny came home; he kissed her softly and crawled in along side as quietly as he could. He wrapped his arm around her. All of the commotion lately had taken such a toll on her, but would be over soon and he'd have his Cherry back in good health. The future was on its way.

She didn't stir when he got up, he let her sleep until after his shower. She and Jenny had plans that morning but a few more minutes wouldn't hurt. She must be completely exhausted, she hadn't move hardly all night long. He showered and came back to wake her with a kiss to her forehead and gentle shake of her shoulder. Cherry didn't respond.

Jenny called the ambulance while Jeff kept trying to wake her, his ability to think fading as his panic grew. In a final rational thought as the sound of the siren approached, he scooped up her pill bottles from the nightstand and yelled for Jenny to find a bag. The hospital would need to know her medications and make sure she had them when she woke up. The look in Jenny's eyes as she held the bag open said it may be necessary for more than that. None were likely lethal by themselves but maybe some combination or maybe too many had done this. She wouldn't have, not on purpose. That was out of the question.

Jenny drove Jeff's car behind the ambulance, nervously trying to follow. She'd reassured her dad everything would be alright as he'd fumbled to find her the keys but, now alone, she tried but didn't believe it. This was bad. The beauty of their talk yesterday played back in a light of being too fortuitous. Things like that happen before a person dies. They somehow know. She fought off the persistent feeling and kept her eyes glued to the road.

She called Sadie from the hospital lobby as tests were beginning on Cherry. Sadie would come as soon as she could. There wasn't anything substantial to know yet, no one knew what had happened or why, but she knew Sadie would want to be told. Jeff thought calling Steve and Bruce should wait until more was known. Steve was coming soon anyway and Bruce was too far away to make the trip, a trip for hopefully no reason. Cherry could come to any minute and be fine.

Sadie arrived just as the lab test results ruled out a medication issue or kidney complication. Bruises had been found on Cherry's leg and upper arm. Did any of them know why? Scans were currently being performed to check for a sign of head trauma, time was of the essence if that had occurred, as it was for bodily internal bleeding. Someone would bring Jeff release forms to sign for procedures pending the findings. That was the extent of the update. There was no false reassurance.

The wait was excruciating, the prognosis getting bleaker with each moment Cherry stayed unconscious. None of them had any idea where she would have gotten bruises. She bruised easily. She may have just gotten them working around the house, a bump here or there against furniture. Sadie hadn't noticed any when she was there; she was the last person to see her. Cherry's clothing may have covered them, depending on just where the bruises were. It didn't really matter now, but the guessing kept other thoughts from taking over their minds.

Sadie stepped outside to call the girls on her cell. There was nothing they could do, and the drive was fairly long for most, but they needed to know as much as she did. Cat's voice mail answered, Sadie left a message just saying to call her as soon as she had a minute. She couldn't bring herself to say the rest and leave Cat in suspense at the whole story. The whole story. There wasn't one. There wasn't a cause, there wasn't a diagnosis, there was no beginning and no end. Just the middle. Just that Cherry was in some kind of apparent coma. Still, they needed to know. They needed to be, if only in thought, by each other's side through this, whatever this turned out to be.

Sydney was silent as Sadie blurted out every detail she knew.

"I want to come," she finally said. "It'll take me a little bit to get on the road, but …"

"It's too far, Syd. I'll call back as soon as I find out anything more. This is just a wait thing now."

"I don't care. I can sit with you if nothing else."

"I'm fine. Sam said he'd come if I want, so I'm okay."

"I'm not. I have to. I'll go nuts here. I'll call the others for you first. Shoot, Maggie's at some doctor's appointment with her mother."

"Try her later, but let me call Wren. I already left a message for Cat. I need something to do. Talk about going nuts."

Sydney agreed to that much but was still going to make the trip. Sadie called Wren and gave her the news. Wren had the same response as Sydney, but the distance made a quick trip out of the question. She'd wait for more news, and thanked Sadie profusely for letting her know. This was so unbelievable. She just won't think the worst yet, she couldn't. How were Jeff and Jenny?

Sadie tried Cat one more time but when it went to voice mail she hung up. Another message would just create alarm. It was just as well Cat hadn't answered because, over her shoulder, Sadie saw Jenny come out the door.

"Anything yet?" Sadie asked.

"Nothing. I just had to get some air."

She moved with Sadie to a nearby bench, immediately resting her head on Sadie's shoulder. Sadie wrapped her arm around her. How open Jenny was. How unlike her mother. Jenny, a mid thirties woman taller than Sadie, allowed herself to curl into the comfort of her mom's long time acquaintance with no hesitation or regard for appearances. Her blondish wild curls looked not brushed yet today. Nick's curls. What a strange thing to think of after all this time, and at this inappropriate moment.

"Yesterday, Mom and I had the most amazing talk," Jenny said, straightening and wiping a tear. "It makes this all the harder. Except in a way easier. Know what I mean?"

"We don't know anything yet. She may come out of this just fine. Want to tell me about your talk?"

Jenny did. Any friend of her mother's was a friend of hers, and no one else was around to listen. Leaving out details to get to its heart, Jenny filled Sadie in on the gist, saying how some insight into her grandmother helped to understand why her mother, following the only way she'd been taught, had raised her like she had.

"Your mom loves you very much. I know that for a fact."

"Me too. After yesterday. My point was now I get it. Wasn't easy before," Jenny said, trying to force a laugh that turned instead to tears. Sadie held her, feeling her own start, until Jenny straightened with a mission.

"I have to get back in with my dad. He must be going crazy."

"I'll go with you."

"I have to stop at the nurse's station. See if they can call the other hospital and cancel tomorrow. Can they do that for us, you think?"

A lump rose in Sadie's throat. "Sure. They'll take care of it."

Jeff was, in fact, going crazy. He was pacing and couldn't stop. He didn't want coffee or any food, he only wanted news, good news, from the doctor. He finally sat when Jenny insisted, then turned to her with a request he felt might have been put off too long, the wait turning him, with each passing minute, against hope.

"We should call the boys. They'd want to be here."

Sadie helped with an offer of her phone. Jenny patted her purse. She had one, and left to contact her brothers.

Sadie slid to the seat next to Jeff and rubbed his back as he hunched forward. She'd known him since college, the soft spoken, skinny boyfriend of Cherry who'd so diligently pursued Cherry with undying love. His balding gray hair and fuller frame now couldn't hide that person, the one so devoted and now hurting in such a different yet similar way.

There wasn't anything to say to comfort him. False hope would be demeaning and empty. She'd barely had time to sort her own feelings. This was Cherry lying so motionless in there. Her Cherry. So happy and normal just last night. Her Cherry, their friendship going all the way back to those same days as Jeff on Highland Street. All the memories, of then and since and in the years of their monthly lunches. She couldn't let them in right now. That would be memorializing them, making them a thing of a distant past and not a part of the present. The present had happened just last night. Cherry just had to be alright.

Jeff reached over and took the hand she now had resting between them. The gesture replaced the words neither had in them to say.

Jenny came back from making her calls with three coffees and cinnamon rolls juggled on a tray. She handed a cup to Jeff and held steady until he took it. Sadie accepted one with thanks and nodded yes to a roll as Jenny bit into hers. Talking to her brothers had obviously helped her mindset.

"Steve's going to leave work and come. Bruce is calling for flights. Said he's hoping for one this aft but if not, if he gets in late, he'll crash at a motel or something so he doesn't wake us up." She looked over at her dad. "If we go home tonight."

He didn't have time for that to sound good or bad, a doctor was approaching their side of the room. The three set down their refreshments in unison and stood.

"Mr. Conlon? I'm Dr. Amery. I've been assisting with diagnosing your wife's condition. It's evident she had a fall of some kind. She has bleeding within the skull area. We directly began draining it to relieve the pressure, it's the only thing we can do, but the success rate generally requires that be done within a much shorter time of the fall. We're doing what we can, I assure you."

"What does all that mean?" Jenny had to know.

"Pressure on the brain for an extended time reduces the ability of function to recover. In her case, we aren't able to know the full range, or if it's retrievable, just yet."

He left with a pat on the shoulder for Jeff and an empathic smile at the two women. Jeff resumed his pacing, seemingly unable or unwilling to fully accept the prognosis.

"When could she have fallen? Where?" His chest rose and fell in struggled breaths. "That's not possible. It doesn't make any sense."

Jenny stood and swung her purse onto her shoulder. "I've got to go make some calls."

Sadie recognized Jenny's real need to be one of just getting out of there, but it left her alone with Jeff. How thankful she was Sydney had insisted on coming. She couldn't do much more of this alone.

She sat. The information had been too much and not enough. Was it wise to hope Cherry would come out of this unscathed and be her normal self again? Thinking any other way went against who Sadie was, but the doctor's words, despite her effort to rewind them with a different and better slant, left little room for optimism.

"She was afraid of dying, you know," Jeff said, in his concentrated pacing.

"Jeff, we don't know anything yet, she…"

"She didn't think I knew how much it bothered her. Ruined a lot of years for her."

"I know. Jeff, she doesn't want Jenny to know, to do that too."

"My God, no. But why did she do that to herself? I never had the nerve to tell her it was stupid. I should have just put my foot down. She could have been happy. She should have."

Sadie stood to pace with him. "It wouldn't have mattered. Trust me. I know her too. It satisfied something in her. It kept her from worrying about something else, maybe you, the kids. I think you did her a favor by not making a big deal out of it. That's why we've always done that too."

"She must be so afraid right now."

Sadie held him as he broke down in her arms, her own tears freed by his.

By the time Jenny came back, they had composed themselves and had reinforced each other's preserving hopes. Jenny was either in a similar state or had talked to someone who was. She had. Her husband was on his way with Daisy. They would coordinate with Bruce and time it to rent a joint car at the airport. They'd come straight to the hospital, all three.

Steven arrived shortly after, and took over as guardian of his father. After a hug for his sister and a nod for Sadie, he listened sympathetically to Jeff's telling of what the doctor had said, then headed for the nurse's station, showing virtually no further emotion. His mother's son, Sadie thought.

"They don't know anything more just yet," he said, returning to sit by Jeff. "You want anything, Pop? A soda, maybe? I bet you haven't eaten. I'll run down to the cafeteria. Anything sound good?"

Jeff shook his head. Steven was off with a wink in Jenny's direction.

"That means he's bringing back food. For all of us, you can bet."

"I think I'll go back outside," Sadie said to her. "Try some calls again."

She needed the break just as Jenny had earlier. Fresh air, new scenery, the stretch a walk provided. She checked her phone. Cat had called. This was going to be hardest one to make. Telling Sydney and Wren had been difficult enough, even when the news hadn't been what it was now. Cat was going to take this badly.

She waited for a spot to clear on the bench. She needed to sit for this as much as Cat would. She fought back tears as Cat answered. Cat, as predicted, did not take it well.

"No! She can't do this! She can't!"

"Listen, can you come up here? I think you should. Syd's on her way. You need to. There's not a thing any of us can do but you need to come for you. And me. And if Cherry wakes up…"

"When Cherry wakes up! When! Yes. I'm coming. I have to go. I have to call Joe. Are you okay? How are you doing?"

"I'm okay. Cat, this is for a reason. Think of that. Promise me."

Maybe it wasn't the best idea to have Cat here at the hospital, but the trip should hopefully give her time to get the bulk of her fire out and rationally regain her philosophic edge. Hopefully.

She debated calling Sam yet. It'd be nice to have his company, but he didn't know Jeff or the family and the wait would be boring for someone not personally involved. Sydney should be here before too long. And Cat. Cat was likely to charter a plane.

In all the commotion of people and calls, Sadie suddenly remembered the reality of Cherry, and felt the pit of her stomach twist in a knot. This had been about her all along but, for the sake of relief, getting sidetracked with things to do had served its purpose of diminishing that reality, a reality now hitting Sadie with a deeply painful stab.

What was Cherry feeling, thinking, at this moment? Was she? With the thought of her being gone impossible to consider, Sadie's mind went to the rest. What if she lives and doesn't know how to function? Or remember all the memories from a lifetime of living? What if she doesn't know who she is?

The doctor could be just giving the worst case scenario. That's what they did in these days of malpractice to cover themselves in case the worst should happen. Cherry could come out of this and be her same self. She could. They could just reschedule the transplant a few weeks down the road after she recovered and regained her strength. This was just like Cherry. Throw a little drama into the mix.

A smile almost crossed Sadie's lips. Then she broke out in shaking sobs.

The waiting room was empty when she returned. No one from anyone's family at all. One had been there for what sounded like a minor bike accident, another for an elderly parent. She took a chair. Asking at the nurses' station wouldn't give any answers. She wasn't family. They wouldn't be able to tell her.

The desperately welcoming sight of Sydney brought her to her feet. The wordless hug let Sydney know there wasn't news, good news, to share. They sat, and Sadie gave her a rundown of the latest, including the quandary of what the missing family might mean.

"They must have gotten some kind of update, I have no idea."

"I'm going to ask. All they can do is say they can't tell me," Sydney said, handing Sadie her purse and starting for the station. Sadie stopped her. Steven had just rounded a corner, his hand searching his breast pocket for probably his phone.

He saw them. "They've transferred her to a room She's in 312." He looked at Sadie's face lighten in hope of that being a hopeful sign, and lowered his eyes against it. "My dad will fill you in." He patted her shoulder and gave Sydney a faint smile before proceeding outside to make his calls.

Sydney, having not been directly involved in the hours of wait, was anxious and questioning on the way to 312. They couldn't jump to any conclusions. They had to stay strong and just hope for the best. Sadie gently stopped her to stand face to face. She'd withheld the depth of the dire prognosis in case it had been wrong, but now had to prepare Sydney for its likelihood. How awful to be a doctor and do this everyday.

They could see through the doorway part of Cherry, her head wrapped in white and her face, her familiar face, partially obscured by an oxygen mask and tubing. Jeff was in a side chair, holding her hand in his. Jenny looked at the two as they started to enter, and came to them, ushering them back to the corridor. Her eyes were puffy, her lips trembling at the words that needed saying.

"They can't find any brain activity." She couldn't look at them any longer than that.

Sydney looked blankly at Sadie, neither yet able to accept what that meant, then took Jenny into her arms and held her. Jenny wouldn't have moved if she'd had a choice but, when Sadie could wait no longer, she patted her shoulder and whispered so both she and Sydney could hear.

"Can we go in and see her, honey? We'll be quiet."

Jenny broke the hold slowly and turned to lead them. "You don't have to be quiet. Maybe your voices will help." Her eyes said she knew they wouldn't.

Jeff looked up as they neared the bed of their longtime beloved sister. She was more than a friend; she was part of each, as much as the family was in a real way. Neither could yet fathom that their Cherry, lying so peacefully in front of their eyes, so perfectly still herself in appearance, could be doing anything but just resting after having a fall. People fell every day. They ended up being alright.

"They're waiting," Jeff mumbled, as Sadie moved to stand by his side. "We're waiting." His eyes moved to the monitor registering all of her vitals. He couldn't say anything else. Jenny started to speak but didn't. There was no reason to take away his last desperate cling to a thread of hope.

Sydney took Cherry's other hand in hers, careful to not disturb the IV taped to the top of it, and gently caressed her fingers. She spoke to her privately, one mind to another, hoping Cherry somehow understood. Don't go, she begged. Please stay. We've come so far together. It's not over yet. There's so much more to do.

"You can talk to her," Jeff said. "Let her hear your voices. If she knows you're here…"

He couldn't finish, but both knew what he meant. Sadie took the lead.

"Syd and I are here, Cher. Cat's coming too. We love you so much. Can you get better for us? For your family? They love you so much too."

"And for yourself," Sydney found a thought she could voice. "You're gonna want to give Cat a hard time when she gets here. You love doing that."

This was too difficult, talking so one sided and keeping it upbeat, not saying what was really in their hearts, especially with Jeff and Jenny in the room. And Steven. He'd just come in from outside.

"Bruce's plane gets in at seven thirty our time. I said I'd pick him up. Jim and Daisy too. Mark and Sheila are on their way. Anyone else, Dad? Want me to call the school for you?"

Jeff seemed to barely hear him. "I did. I can't think of anyone else."

"Syd," Sadie said quietly. "We should do that too. Maggie and Wren." She glanced at Jeff and softened it. "Let them know how she's doing."

Sydney understood it was partly a cue to leave, and was just as anxious as Sadie. They weaved their way out into the hall and headed without speaking to the elevator. Sadie had to get outside to her bench, her one spot of refuge than had so quickly become home for the day. Sydney needed time to have this sink in and make sense.

The elevator doors opened and there stood a panicked Cat, her eyes wild with anticipation of what was to come. They convinced her, in the short time it took for the doors to close, to come with them and they'd explain.

Sadie had been right. The trip had helped Cat gather her wits and find the solace of her sustaining beliefs. That hadn't come without guilt and remorse, she should have done more to save their

Cherry from her self imposed delusions of dying, even though she too, like the rest, had excused the notion as temporary and not seriously true. But this was Cherry's journey, her choice. Her fear had overridden any newfound hope, something she wasn't used to fully absorbing. Sydney listened and let her be. This was no time to argue, and if it helped Cat get through this, fine. For Sadie, Cat's talk brought the first real calm of the day.

Cat went up alone and somehow convinced the ring leader Steven to take his sister and dad for refreshments. What she said to Cherry in those private minutes would forever remain between them, and whether or not Cherry heard at a physical level mattered not to Cat at all. Cherry's soul had heard and talked back. Together they squared their lifetime of loving conflict and made a peace that would carry them until they saw each other again. Until then, Cat promised to talk everyday, so Cherry was not to worry about ever getting lonesome. That much she later shared with the others, an effort to have them promise the same. They did.

Evening brought the rest of the family, so Sadie invited Sydney and Cat back to her house to wait. They'd talked to Jenny and knew the still tentative but inevitable plan. Staying at the hospital until then wouldn't help Cherry or the others, and not their own grief either. They left to spend a restless night and returned early the next morning.

The third floor waiting room held apparent spouses and children, Cherry's grandchildren, nieces or nephew, children they had vicariously watched grow through Cherry's funny and loving tales. This wasn't the time for introductions. They made their way to room 312. Jenny was the first to see them in the doorway and motioned them to come inside. Cherry lay peacefully, all signs of life support removed from her. Bruce and Steven stood aside their father on one side of the bed, Jenny nestled back into her Uncle Mark's arms on the other. The girls took places at the bed's foot, silently watching their beloved Cherry breathing on her own.

At first it seemed she should wake any second, just blink or open her eyes. They knew better, but the horrific reality of standing there, watching and waiting, had to be countered to make it bearable. They saw in her face the Cherry they knew, the young girl with the hope of finding a husband and having a life of family and friends. She'd accomplished that, she'd accomplished what she'd set out to do so long ago and yet seeming like merely yesterday. All the fun times on Highland. She had been so integral to their life there, all her cleaning and hair fussing and perfectly timed jokes. She was always one step off norm, even at all the reunions since and times in between. It made her who she was. It made her belong. They wouldn't have been who they were without her.

They wouldn't ever recall their exact thoughts as each relinquished and said a special goodbye. Cat, in the middle, took Sadie and Sydney's hands in hers. Cherry's breathing was slowing, becoming almost too shallow to see. And then, on this morning of what was to have been the day of her new beginning, Cherry gave up the last fight of her life.

Chapter 14

Jeff had asked the women to sit with the family in the first few rows of pews at the service. He was being polite but also needed them close. They were as much a part of his Cherry as the children she had given him. They were a safety net of sorts, a comfort where no comfort existed.

Maggie had assured Jay, and Sydney her Dan, they'd be alright attending the funeral without them. They'd stay at Sadie's, they would have each other. Both men reluctantly agreed. They fully understood their wives, and had participated on the edge at reunions enough to know the women right now most needed one another. Cat's Joe, even without that background, knew the same. They would get their chance to help in the weeks and months ahead, as the initial grief would surely turn to a deep, yet healing, sorrow.

The five were staying at Sadie's cottage home, bunking wherever there was room. A motel was rather close by but not considered in their need to be together, the tighter, the better. They'd stayed up into the middle of the night, alternating shower times to avoid a morning run on the bathroom, and talking, sometimes around, sometimes in depth, about Cherry. Sadie recounted the final days in such detail they felt they had been there. They'd wanted and needed to know.

Jenny had called, she'd found the place of the fall the day before the funeral as she'd rounded up her clothes from the laundry. It wasn't like her meticulous mother to have scattered items in corners, some in plain sight, or a load left unattended in the washer. She must have been afraid or unable to come back down to switch it. If it hadn't been for that stupid movie, if her dad and she had been home, her mom would very possibly still be alive.

Jeff too was taking on his guilt and what ifs, she'd said. She didn't know how to help him. Privately, Sadie was dealing with some of her own, despite trying to believe as Cat did that this all was Cherry's choice on some level. Still, if she'd gone that night earlier, if she'd stayed longer, if she hadn't gone at all, the timing for Cherry doing the laundry would have been different or maybe she wouldn't have done at all. Futile thoughts but there.

Cat's premise that Cherry couldn't, in the end, justify the transplant using Jenny had a valid ring, far-fetched as it sounded to some. Ludicrous, in fact, to Sydney, an opinion she again kept to herself. If continually talking like this was what Cat had to do to cope, who was she to disagree. When it came to such ethereal matters, there wasn't really wrong or right. Because of all that and on the slim to none chance Cat had a point, she withheld any otherwise comment.

For one, she knew Cat. Cat wasn't internalizing this, she was rationalizing it away under the guise of beliefs to avoid the pain connected. She and Cherry, in their strange rapport, had too much of a history for this to be brushed aside as simply part of life's mystery. Cat could only grasp this by picking it apart, and when there were no more pieces to intertwine, Cat would likely come undone. Hopefully that wouldn't happen until after church.

Jeff had appeared to be holding up well when he'd greeted his and Cherry's friends at the wake. Jenny too. She hadn't worn make-up, maybe thinking it'd be useless, but was dressed very nicely in black. She introduced her husband and Daisy to the girls, and pointed out a few people special to Cherry. The girls had then been on their own and they'd stayed just appropriately long. As much as they'd like to learn more of Cherry through her and Jeff's outside friends, the circumstance made that too difficult.

The church began to fill to capacity, most probably the same groups as last night. Cherry would have been so pleased. Many were from Jeff's school, others likely church members since Cherry had been so actively involved. It'd been her one refuge, besides work and the girls, from the often taxing stress of the family, and didn't demand more from her than she was willing to give. The girls were glad she'd had that. It seemed a very nice fit.

They paid their last respects to her as most began talking their seats. Sadie, Cat, and Sydney had had at least some foresight of this, but for Maggie and Wren it was even more gut wrenching. Saying she looked lovely, as so many had, wasn't the sentiment any was feeling. She was lifeless. She was gone. In a minute they would have nothing but pictures and memories and right now those seemed empty at best. They clung to each other protecting Maggie and Wren, but none were able to absorb its reality. They stepped aside as the family neared for their turn. None took a final long lasting look. They just couldn't call that the end.

Some were faintly aware of the whispers as they followed the closed casket and family down the aisle to the front of the church. The children with spouses were rather identifiable; five single women all the same age could probably be pegged as old school chums or out of town friends. Cherry or Jeff may have spoken of them so perhaps some knew who they were. A sense of honor helped distract them from the anguish of the walk, a last walk with one of their own. Friendship was, all week long, taking on a new meaning.

The opening service was rather soothing, the unfamiliar surroundings and minister's quaint ways drawing attention and giving intermittent respite from the reason for the gathering. When he spoke, it was obvious he had known Cherry quite well, liked her and respected her and Jeff. He spoke highly of her commitment to the church, doing his best to interject bits of humor to alleviate everyone's pain. Her customary habit of staying at a bake sale until the last penny had been counted and the left goodies divided was selfless unless you knew her, he said fondly. Nothing tripped her trigger, those were his words, like a free piece of blueberry pie. There were moments when his created visions of her were so vivid, so true, it was stabbing to then remember she no longer was here.

Steven next spoke for the family, a rather factual account of his mother as a loving wife, mother, a member of the church and community. Understandably, the minister was a hard act to follow, but Steven's unemotional and dull recital of words did not seem to properly eulogize a mother he obviously had really adored. He looked up from his notes at the end, his feelings starting to free themselves, and added an impromptu closing.

"I know most of you knew my mother in one capacity or another from here in town. She was many things to many people, and she would match herself to whatever the circumstances called for. If she was cheering at one of our games, she could drown out the whole bleacher. If she was sitting for hours at a nursing home, reading quietly to the elderly, she did that. When I needed a kick to do my homework, she could do it harder than anybody I know. Not literally, of course. But she got the job done. And then she'd give me a homemade cookie and a kiss to the top of my head. When any of us gave her reason to worry, and we did, she'd scold and yell like a trouper. She never knew we'd see her secretly cry."

He stopped at the sound of a soft guttural wail, coming from the row behind his father, and gave the two women comforting one between them a moment to do their consoling.

Cat was coming undone.

"There is something, though, most of you probably don't know about my mother," Steven continued. "She had a group of friends from college. They weren't just friends. They were like sisters. They meant everything to her. They were the ones who gave her the strength to get through every difficultly she ever faced. She always told us," he looked at the five women in question. "That if one of you called, we were to tell her, even if she was in the garden up to her elbows in dirt. Or in the middle of taking a shower. You five were her lifeline to being a person, not just a wife and mother. She belonged to you as much as to our family. She loved God, she loved my dad and us, and she loved each one of you."

He gathered his notes and stepped down from the pulpit. Cat freed herself from the wrap of Sydney and Wren and made her way to him in the aisle. She hugged him with everything she had in her, sobbing wordlessly into his shoulder. He hugged her in return, his first tears falling silently onto her. The scene brought some in the church to release quiet cries of their own, others, primarily the other four seated women, watching and not daring to breathe.

All was well. Cat had just needed to do that. She took her seat unapologetically and accepted Sydney's warm arm again.

The minister, in all of his professional and personal graciousness, led the congregation in a heartfelt and uplifting prayer. Cherry was now an angel, happy and safe in God's company. All of her earthly boundaries and burdens had been lifted from her sturdy shoulders. It was her time for her heavenly reward, and while she was enjoying it, she would be watching over her loved ones, anxious for the day they would all meet again.

He raised his head with a gentle smile and gave a slight wave to the organist. That was Sadie's cue too. She made her way to the front. When Jeff had asked if she'd be willing to do this, saying Cherry would have liked it so much, she'd quickly agreed and said she'd be honored. Standing now, waiting for the moment to begin, Sadie wasn't sure she could. The minister's words had helped put a momentary fix on death and dying, a feeling that had lasted until she'd come up here so near the casket. Cherry, not death and dying, was within feet. Her body, Sadie told herself, not her, but still, she couldn't look at it.

She knew the song by heart. She'd been called on to sing it so many times at churches she didn't belong to for people she didn't know. The word just seemed to have spread. The organist now nodded. Sadie began. Her voice sang out a cappella, its purity causing complete silence of any other sound in the church.

Amazing Grace, how sweet the sound,

That saved a wretch like me.

I once was lost but now am found,

Was blind, but now I see.

As the organ joined in and the fullness of the music took hold, Sadie fought to steady her voice. She had to keep going, she had to get through, she had to do it for Cherry.

Maggie stood, then instantly Wren, Cat and Sydney, and together they single filed to the front to cluster around Sadie as if planned, arms around each other's waists. Sadie's voice now joined theirs. She found again her clarity and will, and now looked over at Cherry. This is for you, she said to herself, knowing Cherry heard.

Either that show of solidarity or Steven's speech made seemingly every person in attendance want to talk to them after the service. They found solace again in the ride to the burial, a solace of unity without many words, only to become separated again as one by one they were pulled into conversations by well meaning friends of Cherry's. They gathered at the newly dug plot, searching in the crowd for each other. Cherry's casket had been discreetly placed on the lowering device before the onlookers arrived. Silence fell as the minister began a prayer.

Sadie heard Cat's unmistakable sobbing somewhere behind her, Cat's grief once again uncontainable. Decorum said to not disturb others, their heads hung in solemn praying, but Cat shouldn't be alone. Sadie moved slightly to her right and then backwards as many steps as room allowed. Wren finally caught her eye, knowing fully why Sadie was concerned, and discreetly pointed to Cat, cradled almost out of sight in her arms.

The graveside service concluded without lowering the casket, a local practice or a formality forsaken out of respect for grievers. The girls each in their place took a last look, then disbursed to the car without lingering, the procession back needing their car to move and the finality too much to bear.

"It's so stupid to go through all that for a body," Cat managed to say, feeling a need to say something. "She's not there, she's right here with us in the car." With that, she once again broke down and buried her head against Maggie.

They had agreed to go back to the church for the luncheon, on the unanimous but silent premise that staying within the organized grief somehow would prolong the emptiness. Normal life seemed eons removed, too far away right now to ever be reached again. The thought of taking Cat in was a bit disconcerting, for her sake as well as others, since she could further erupt at any moment and her tendency to not care what she said or who was around could present a problem. But by the time the procession arrived back at the church, she'd seemed to have regained control.

"Come on. Let's do this fucker," she said, prodding Maggie to get out of the car.

Complete control was asking too much.

They mingled, separating again as they did so but had reserved a table to meet. They each eventually made their way through the food line and came together to sit.

"Sadie, did you ever meet her boss? Is he here?" Maggie asked.

"No, I didn't. And I don't know what he looks like either. Could be any of these guys."

"It's probably not a good idea to ask Jeff," Sydney said. "That'd be kind of tacky, don't you think?"

They quickly agreed and let it drop since Steven was approaching their table.

"I just want to thank you all for coming. I'm pretty sure for some of you it was a fairly good distance."

Sadie realized he wouldn't have ever had reason or opportunity to actually meet most of them. She began a round of introductions.

"Sadie's been at the house a few times when I've been home," he said to explain knowing her. "And Cat, Catherine, isn't it? You I remember from a time when I was a teenager."

"Cat's good," Cat said. "And good memory. I came for your mom's birthday one year. Just to surprise her. Thanks for all that you said this morning. It meant a lot."

"Well, you all meant a lot to her. It's me who should thank you."

"Yeah, we did," Cat said. "Still, it was a helleva nice gesture. You did good."

Steven took a fake half bow. "Thank you. I sensed your appreciation already." He looked her in the eyes warmly, trying to say just how much it had meant. Then he laughed and gave her a wink. "I get some of my mother's stories now."

"How's your dad doing?" Sydney asked.

"He's holding up." That with a deep breath. "He's taking it hard, but he'll be better with time."

"I don't know about that," Cat said.

Steven looked surprised. "It won't be easy for him, that's for sure. These things never are, but…"

"We've known him since before they got married. He's not going to be fine, probably not ever." Cat saw no reason to sugar coat it.

The others quickly tried to retract the harshness, reassuring Steven his father could manage. It was too little too late, but could have been for the best. In the awkward few moments it took to listen, he understood more than a lifetime with his parents had shown. These women, these virtual strangers, had been in his parents' lives longer than he had. They had known them as young people, growing into their selves, their foibles and flaws and apparently the secrets of their love for one another. It'd be interesting to learn more, but he also fully knew he would have had to be there to truly understand. What he saw just from this much, though, was his father, for the first time, as a person.

"I'll certainly do what I can for him, I promise," he said. "Would it be okay for him to call one of you once in awhile? Or you call him? I think that would help a great deal."

"Of course," Sydney said. "That a very good idea. We will. We'll keep tabs on him. Do what we can."

Steven thanked them and left, moved by the awe he'd felt in their presence. If he had to do all over again, he'd have run faster, yelled louder, when one of them had phoned for his mother.

The room began to clear, leaving just stragglers, the girls, and the family.

"This is it?" Cat said rather loudly. "This is how a whole life just ends? Everybody just goes back to what they were doing?"

Sydney's patience was nearing its end. "Of course not. Is it over for you?"

"Feels like it's just beginning."

"There you go. Come on, let's help pick up a little."

The activity felt good. It gave them something to do and the chance to burn off more unused disquiet. A few church workers said their help wasn't necessary, but were grateful nonetheless. Avoiding the area of still seated family and relatives or friends, they all took tables by twos and cleared the well worn ceramic plates, cups, and utensils. For Sadie, it was such a flashback to years as a teen and her own family's church functions. Some things seemed never to vary or change. If only today's cause for being here hadn't happened. It so drastically changed so much.

Jeff was in the kitchen, thanking the church women there for all they had done. Cherry would have so appreciated it. He knew she was looking down and watching. One put her arm around him, another patted his shoulder but kept up her work. This wasn't the first funeral they'd served, nor would it be the last, yet each one carried a special sadness. The ones for the elderly weren't so bad, but were for a young person, and for a person like Cherry they knew well and liked.

He turned to see Wren and Sydney come in with a load of dishes for the washer. "Oh, you don't have to do that."

"We know," Wren smiled. "We want to."

Sadie and Maggie came in with theirs, announcing Cat had pooped out on helping and was sitting down visiting. Before any could head back out, Jeff motioned them off to a private corner and faced them with a request.

"You've all done so much already, I hate to even ask. It's just that I'm worried about Jenny. She needs... I don't know, maybe a woman to talk to. I was wondering if maybe one of you could talk to her? Maybe keep in touch?"

"Of course," Maggie said. "We'd be happy to. This has to be so hard for her."

"It is." Jeff shook his head. "She's doing her best to look like she's coping, but I know her. The night before... she told me she had a nice talk with her mom... they had their rough spots, as you probably know, it sounded like they kind of mended some real fences. If that somehow is making this worse... I just can't see how that could be, but I don't know. All I know is she's really hurting, and she won't talk to me. She does, I mean, but just about things like arrangements, practical things."

"She knows this is hard for you too," Sydney said. "She's probably protecting you by trying to stay strong."

"Oh, I'm sure. But I want to help her just as much. She wouldn't let me. She clams up when I try, like I wouldn't be any help anyway."

"I'm sure she just doesn't want to add to what you're going through," soothed Wren.

"Still," he said, his words polite but his face pleading. "If one of you wouldn't mind, I just think she needs somebody to talk to. She's keeping this too bottled up. It's not healthy for her."

"You don't suppose," Maggie carefully ventured, "that when she and Cherry had their talk, that Cherry might have... finally told her?"

Jeff looked confused. "Told her?"

She'd started this, but hadn't expected to have to say it. "About Jenny's real... her conception."

"No, no, I'm sure she didn't. Positive. She was always was adamant about that. She said if Jenny ever knew she'd come from rape, she'd feel like she didn't belong. No, there'd be no way she'd have told her."

As surprised as the girls were at the insinuation of rape, it immediately became not the most pressing concern.

Jenny was standing in the doorway.

Chapter 15

The quiet rippling of the river on the edge of Sadie's yard belied the tumultuous mood of the gathering. The five sat, talking at once and then falling silent, each consumed with individual thoughts. The last hour at the church had all but erased their grieving, if only for this immediate afternoon. In its place, having a misery of its own, was the looming issue at hand.

They had stayed long enough to help Jeff ease an insistent Jenny to a table, and had backed him as he'd told her the truth. The truth as he knew it. Her birth was a result of her mother being raped.

"We have to let it go. We can't interfere," Sydney said. "It's just not our place."

Maggie was still taking blame. "If I just hadn't said that. Where in the world was my head? I can't remember why bringing it up could have remotely been logical to what we were talking about."

"Because it was," Wren said in support. "It dawned on me too."

"It really was Jeff who gave it away," added Sadie. "He's the one who actually said it."

"Guess for once you guys can't pin it on me. I wasn't even there."

"Give us time, Cat," said Sydney. "We'll figure a way."

"You should have been keeping her entertained or something," teased Sadie.

"See? But anyway. Poor Cherry has to be rolling over. She went all those years without telling and then, poof, before she's even in the ground it comes out. To the whole family, no less. How ironic is that?"

Disrespectful as that sounded, it was true. It also meant Cat was maybe slightly healing.

A befuddled Jeff, so in shock of having to handle this, especially on this day, actually had risen to the occasion with caring strength. He was her father in every sense, he assured Jenny. He'd loved her as his own from before she was born. And it'd been out of tremendous love that her mother had kept it from her. She'd wanted to protect her and have her life be normal, never worrying or wondering about anything more.

The brothers and others in the immediate family had walked over midway through to see what was going on, and Jeff caught them up with the same tender finesse. He included them in the great love Cherry had for her children, and her efforts to always do what was best. He took them back to the day she'd confessed to that pregnancy and how she hadn't shown any bitterness. She'd come out of the traumatic ordeal with no thought for herself, just resolve to raise the child, and any others she'd someday be blessed with, in a loving home. As much as he'd loved her before, he loved her more from the moment he knew. Jenny and the boys were equal in his eyes, as they had been in their mother's, a strong, beautiful mother who'd lived for their family's happiness.

Jenny had sat quietly, seeming to absorb and yet not hearing any of it. She declined Jeff's suggestion to go home with the Highland group if she wanted to talk, rather a relief to the group. They weren't prepared. The story had come as a shock to them too. They had to discuss it as a united front if any were to be of help to Jenny. She chose instead to go to the hotel with her husband and daughter, and would see Jeff later. She wasn't angry, she wasn't rude, she even bent to kiss his forehead as she rose to leave, she simply had no more to say.

"I think, once it soaks in," Sadie offered now to the gathering in the yard. "It's going to answer a lot of questions. It should, anyway. About her relationship with her mom."

"I don't think it was bad really, their relationship," Wren said. "Cherry's stories were kind of cute, like Jenny was just a handful."

"I always thought that too," said Sadie, "until some of our lunches. She kind of opened up about how some of it was pretty hard. It sounded like at one point she and Jenny didn't speak for over a year. But Jenny told me they had a nice talk last week, resolved a lot."

"I keep going back to that last semester at school. Again. I did when she told us about Nick, too." Wren was off on another track. "She'd have been pregnant for almost two months before she and Jeff said they were getting married. I slept in the same room with her. She never said a word. She must have been so scared, wondering what to do. I just wish she'd have confided in me. It must have been too hard."

"I wish we'd known all this when we pushed her to tell Jenny," Sydney said, peeved at the deceit regardless the circumstances. "Obviously that was wasted breathe."

Maggie was fighting to find some redeeming aspect of this. "Did you guys think Jeff seemed kind of relieved to have this out? I mean, I'm sure not then and there, but he handled it like he'd been rehearsing for years. I just wonder. All this time it's been his secret too."

Sydney was also thinking of that now, but in a different way. "The only thing is, even he doesn't know the whole story. I'm not sure we should let him, or Jenny, keep thinking it was rape. Especially since we know who he is."

"I don't know. Makes Cherry seem more like a victim to have gone through that, not that being a victim is a good thing, but she'd think so," Cat said. "Preserves her good name. It's still a lie, but what good would it do to have Jenny know it was really a hot one night stand?"

"We don't know that," said Maggie. "I think, looking back at the way she talked about Nick, she could have been in love with him."

"She was." Sadie again with her inside knowledge.

"I take it back anyway," Cat said. "Syd's right. If we don't give it to her straight, we can't tell her we know who the guy is."

"I'm not sure she has to find out," Maggie said. "There are people born of real rape who never do. Does it really matter? And think what it'd do to Jeff to know she lied. He'd be absolutely devastated."

"The other thing is, what do we know, really?" Wren got up to stretch and think. "We weren't there. Sadie, she could have been covering up to you, to us, as easily as she did to Jeff. Maybe she and Nick were together, but then something else happened. Maybe both stories are true. She might not have known who the father was for sure. We can't know."

"Okay." Cat turned to Sydney. "Your opinion. What do you think by looking at Jenny?"

Sydney paused. "I'd say she's Nick's. Just by looks, I'd say probably yes."

"How was it to see her?" Wren asked her, sitting again.

"Kind of weird. And it was a little distracting with her right in front of me through the whole service. Yeah. Kind of weird."

"It seems strange to me Jeff never had Cherry report it, or try to go after the guy," Maggie said.

Cat laughed. "You ever argue with her?"

"We don't know that they didn't," Wren said, again trying to reason all angles. "He just told Jenny they never found out who it was."

"They didn't report anything, that much I bet. We'd have had cops at the house if they had." Then Cat caught their sideways glances. "For her. Assholes."

Sydney stood to get a drink. "I still have the hardest time believing you married a judge."

Cat got up without a word and headed for the bank of the water.

"Cat, I'm sorry. I was kidding."

"Let her be," Wren said calmly. "It's not that. She's just trying to deal."

Wren was right. They watched as Cat stood motionless, staring at the water, the memories of the old days, the beginning, crowding in as if they were immediate reality. Sydney went to stand by her side just as Cat sank to her knees in sorrow.

"She shouldn't have!" Cat cried. "She didn't have to go!"

"Honey, honey." Sydney bent to cradle her. "You always say everybody has their own journey. She knew that, she did. There wasn't anything any of us could have done to change things."

"I tried." Cat was inconsolable, and as she freely let her grief flow, Sydney, and now the others joining them, let theirs go as well. None had cried, not even Sadie, not a cry of any cleansing merit. They did so now, clinging to each other. The depth of it had finally sunk in, and their wrenching ache for the loss of Cherry was also for the part of themselves, in the scope of their dynamics, that had died with her.

What had started so long ago as friendship, born out of mutual bonding, had grown over the years to become so much more. They had seen each other through tribulations on Highland that none could have predicted, trials that had changed them from friends to a dependent unity of one, rooted as such from the start but flowering when they branched into adulthood. To now. Now they had to carry on minus the likes of a vital organ.

Cherry had been such a loud presence, her winsome direness an equalizing force. It had been Cherry who'd help keep their dreams in check, was the first to spot a danger. For better or worse, she'd always been on hand to offer her take, serving as a body guard of sorts, protecting them against the unknown. Above all else, through Cherry and her ways they had learned how to think more openly for themselves, and in doing that and everything else had helped them become the individuals and group of today.

As they made their way back to the cottage, Sadie turned to the spot they had stood. "I'm going to plant a tree right there," she said. Within a few days, she had.

They parted for the time being later that afternoon, having come to a decision on Jenny. In the end, there was no debate. Cherry had entrusted them with her secret. It wasn't theirs to share. Jeff and Jenny had reconnecting to do and, although the truth may or may not have aided in that, no harm would come from withholding. Cherry's utmost objective had been to protect both her husband and daughter from the pain it would cause either to know. There seemed no choice but to adhere to her wishes and hope it was the right thing to do.

They left in pairs, Sydney and Maggie going back to the coast and Wren and Cat south to their cities, which left Sadie the only one there when the call came that evening from Jenny. Yes, Sadie would welcome a visit. She understood Jenny needed to talk.

"I just want to know what you know," Jenny said quietly, accepting a tea from Sadie at the kitchen table. "You knew her probably more than my dad. Jeff."

"He's your dad, Jen. Go ahead and call him that. He's your dad in the way that matters. I've never known a more dedicated father. I know all this has to be a shock, at such a horrible time, but he is."

"She ran the house, though. Just like my grandma did. My grandpa was the same way as him."

"Well, a lot of times you marry what you know."

"I didn't. In fact, I worked hard not to."

"All I know is what I saw in the early days when they were dating. He did the chasing. He was so in love. He knew exactly what your mom was like and she's who he wanted. That's a sign of a pretty strong guy, if you ask me."

"Maybe so, but all I've ever seen is him being, I don't know, kind of a wuss. Submissive. I was thinking on the way over here, do you think he was always trying to make up for what happened to her?"

Sadie had to swallow the words so close to the tip of her tongue. "I think, yes, in a way. He understood that's what she needed, so that's what he was. He did it out of love, not weakness. That's what I think."

"I guess. I really shouldn't fault him, he's been pretty good to me, especially under the circumstances. I wonder if he ever wanted to tell me, and she said no."

"Ask him. Have you talked to him?"

"No, I need some time for this to add up. You know, it kind of does, in some strange way. Can't really explain it. It just does."

"I do know that your mother was protecting you by not telling. She was so afraid it would leave you feeling different, unwanted, something. Or that you'd hate her. She meant well, she did."

"Why would I hate her? It wasn't her fault. I just don't get any of it. I'd have done fine knowing. I would have."

This was trickier than Sadie had expected. "From what I know, from what she said, at first she was waiting for the right time, then as each year went by, it just got harder to face. She thought you'd wonder why she waited. Then it felt too late." Sadie was filling in some as she went, but it sounded like Cherry and made sense. "Tell me about it adding up, though. Now that you know."

"I used to think she just didn't like me. She was so strict, almost mean, it felt like. I know it was how she was raised, but still. Now I bet it wasn't just that, or me, it was that I reminded her of what happened."

Sadie wasn't sure it was right to let that go unanswered but words were momentarily failing her. So much more was involved in this than she and the others had anticipated. What a wide web secrets cast. She got up to refill their tea.

"I wish I could tell her I understand," Jenny continued, needing to talk as much as get information. "We were just getting to know each other. That talk that afternoon. It blew me away." She fought back tears. "I just wish she would have told me, even then, so I could let her know it was okay. That I still loved her. Even more."

Sadie gave her a hug with a free arm as she poured the cups. "I know, sweetie. I know. You know what I would do if I was you? Talk to her. Just tell her. I happen to firmly believe she'll hear you. I've been talking to her. It works. Really."

Jenny nodded and collected herself as Sadie sat again. "I will. For one thing, I'll get to finish without her pooh-poohing me." That with a managed grin.

Sadie laughed. It was time for stories of the days back on Highland when Cherry was at her outrageously finest. If Jenny thought she had it rough, she should have been under the rules of Cherry as their self appointed house mother. The brief lightness, brief since neither was ready, was still refreshing, and served to join their private losses. Hearing of her mother as a young, vibrant woman was so new to Jenny, so unfamiliar and nice, until again the matter of rape surfaced amidst the remembrance.

"She didn't tell any of you?"

"Not then, not for years. She just announced she and your dad were getting married after graduation, and that she was pregnant. We seriously didn't have a clue." That, at least, was the whole truth.

"When did she? When did you know?"

"At one of the reunions. She'd carried it alone… I mean, besides with your dad… for so long, it just got too heavy. She needed our support. We all shared things like that, we trusted each other. We actually tried to convince her to tell you, but, like I said, she was afraid it was too late."

Jenny was silent for a moment. "You know where she got that, don't you? That, that dirty laundry secret keeping? Her mother. Her mother was a piece of work."

"You know, for as highly as your mom always spoke of her, I wondered about that."

The whole story of the near drowning came out, with the

punishment in all of its twisted horror. Sadie was agape, as devastated and aware as Jenny of the repercussion that had then shaped Cherry's life.

"I know she was your grandmother, Jen, but this just turns my stomach. I'm sorry."

"Don't be. I feel the same way. The sickest part, one of them anyway, is when I said I hated her, my mom defended her. That's the impact the witch made."

The sad fact of it silenced them both.

"I'm so pissed off I can hardly stand it!" Sadie got up to do something, anything. She went for the teapot. "I get it, and you're right, but it makes me furious."

All of Cherry's obsessive ways and fanatic quirks were no longer humorous in this light. Cherry was petrified of everything. Of germs, of failing, her hair, right and wrong, of anything not perfect. Sadie had a flashing thought. How extra hard that must have made the admittance to embezzling. The embezzling may have been her desire to free herself. Incorrectly, but at least an attempt. This wasn't the time to figure that out, but she couldn't wait to call the girls.

"Me too. Look what it did to my life. You know what else? I bet it's what made the rape so impossible to talk about, now that I think about it. She must have seen it as not being a good girl. Geez. Poor Mom. What a horrendous thing to do to a person. A child."

Nick. He may have been her first attempt. If so, and it had ended in pregnancy, she must have retreated in more shame and guilt than any of them could have guessed. Sadie slammed down the pot on the table.

"I agree."

"What a heritage. I was just thinking, how much worse could my other half be? Just what I need. Add a slimy psychopath rapist to the list. I probably don't even want to know."

Sadie sat and leaned forward, grasping Jenny's hand. "You're not anyone but yourself. Look at how you've turned out. You've taken the past and turned it around and you're fine. You're amazing. As far as the guy, my bet is he was just a horny college kid. Your mom, she wasn't much of drinker but she always tried to keep up. I'd put money on the fact she just got blitzed at some party and somebody took advantage. It happens. Anyway, what does it matter now? You are you. You're here because you were meant to be born. That's how I see it."

"Thanks," Jenny said, squeezing Sadie's hand. "You're cool. My mom was lucky to have you."

"She was luckier to have you."

"Well, aren't we something?" Jenny chuckled, rising to take her leave.

Sadie smiled. "We certainly are! Listen, I know today has been overload for you, and I can't begin to imagine what you're going through with all of it. But if it helps, I think the best way to honor your mom, and come to some terms with this part, actually everything, is to let your dad be your dad. It's what she wanted for you. She thought she was doing the right thing because of who he is. He can help, he really can."

Jenny reached for a hug. "I know."

"I'm always here too, we all are. Anytime you want to talk."

An idea was forming for Sadie, unspoken that night but coming to fruition at the reunion less than four months later. They invited Jenny. It was too soon, emotions yet too raw, to hold their standard ritual, still they couldn't let that fall slide without one. Changing things up a bit was in order, and Jenny, along with Jeff, was the perfect answer.

The pieces began to come together rather inadvertently. In first deciding on ways to make it bearable, they decided to include their husbands. Just this time. That had been Sydney's idea, a good one especially for Sadie, since bringing her significant Sam helped relieve memories of sharing for years the ride with Cherry. And when Jenny called to say she was coming back home to help her father let go of Cherry's things, extending an invitation to them seemed to top off this reunion's intent.

Friday afternoon belonged just to the girls, the guys went golfing and Jeff and Jenny weren't coming until morning. They sat on Sydney's deck, all of them the same and yet so changed. For all the thoughts of this being empty without Cherry, it quickly became clear she was more present than ever. She, minus what she had always brought to the table, was with them and was the focus of talk.

Sadie's immediate calls of the near drowning had been the filter through which each was beginning to heal. It put into perspective the way Cherry had been and helped to soothe the rough edges of an otherwise glorified remembrance. The question of how things may have gone if any had known and could have somehow alleviated the incident's residue was left alone as a now useless sentiment. Still, each in their own minds thought it, and wished with all their hearts they could somehow make retribution.

"I wanted to surprise you guys," Sydney said. "Guess what? I'm putting my name on the living donor list. To give a kidney."

"How wonderful!"

"Are you sure?"

"Way to go!"

"What a tribute!"

"Yes, I'm sure, and yes, it's my tribute to her. It's actually for a lot of reasons, one being that it makes me feel good. Seems funny that being selfless can be selfish. Or something like that. It's just that, man, the shock of how fast it can end, how a life can just be over, I wanted mine to matter in a bigger way than it has so far."

"You matter plenty, Syd. I couldn't imagine not having you in my life," said Wren. But I know what you're saying. And how fragile it is. It's still just so hard to know she's not going to call or, like now, pull up in the driveway and tell us we should have waited for her. It doesn't seem possible she, like, disappeared."

"She's not gone," Cat said. "She's in us."

"Yes, but not her presence," said Maggie. "She's not here telling us some story, or talking about the old days with us. She loved to do that."

"And slanting the facts." Cat then caught all eyes on her. "Well, she did. It's okay, it was part of her. The truth."

Wren got it and smiled. "Or tell us we'd go to hell for talking about her."

That opened a round of loving but honest stories of Cherry's often intrusive ways, something they hadn't expected to flow so freely quite yet. But Cat was right, it was who she was, the reason apparent or not and forgivable. It helped in seeing her, feeling her, admitting her place in the group. And so began the letting go of her with respect and gratitude, and hope for the remaining unity to continue, changed yet still the same.

"I almost forgot," Sadie said. "Sam just got word from the insurance board. They've got her boss on big time violations. He's getting charged!"

It had started as a tribute in much the same way as Sydney's, done to honor Cherry's memory. Sadie had asked Sam to pose as a prospective client to catch Glenn at his ways, a bit unsure of what was true but suspecting Cherry was right. Sam did some research and went into it armed, playing a game of hesitancy until the agent buckled and offered him part of his commission, a serious infraction and enough to warrant an inquest into office policies.

Even though she'd started it, the direction of the probe had sent waves of anxiety through Sadie. She'd hoped she'd done the right thing. If Glenn really had the dummy accounts, the ones where Cherry's refund could be detected, the issue of having dummies at all should override any activity within them. It did, and took down the accountants as well. In light of primary violations, the issue of juggling money seemed to be covered by the fact each accountant had rather recently received a bonus of five thousand dollars, Glenn a thousand, determined to have been squirreled from the dummies with no intensive delving. Glenn, to his credit or maybe to avoid worse damage, conceded to the charges before any involvement of the deceased secretary rendered an opinion other than she'd been an indirect, hapless, and unknowing pawn.

"But that's it," she said. "I'm never, never, doing something like that again. My nerves can't take the suspense. Don't anybody tell me you've broken the law because you'll be on your own. I swear."

"Crap. I really needed a witness to say I was at your house yesterday," teased Cat. "When Joe's car got that ding in the front."

"Good job, Sadie," Sydney said. The rest chimed in with their kudos.

They talked all afternoon about the Cherry that belonged solely to them, realizing that tomorrow when Jeff and Jenny came, the conversation needed to be clear of portions. That embezzling for one, Jenny's birth father, and intimate exchanges from past reunions that gave clues to a private Cherry her family wouldn't benefit from knowing. Her embattled quest for acceptance, her lackluster sex life with Jeff. The transparency in her details of a fantasy childhood, ones they so wished they had been able to see before now. Leaving hindsight where it belonged, they hashed over with love the Cherry they knew.

Amidst the melancholy of old remembrances, they five began to heal. It would take time, much more than a few months, for Cherry's life and death to find a restful place in their hearts, but by that evening they were one good day closer and ready to meet the men for an enjoyable dinner on the veranda at Shrimp N' Mugs. The usual Friday night lobster boil had been intentionally moved to Saturday, in part to break tradition this time and in part to include Jeff and Jenny. The busy work of setting it up would get everyone involved, and give those unfamiliar with the feast a taste of rituals past.

"She talked about this part after every time," said Jeff, sitting down in his chair with a cob of corn. "Sydney, this is so nice. Your place is so nice. Thank you for sharing it with her."

"And with us," Jenny added.

"If I'd known it was like this," Cat's Joe said, nodding at the boiling pot of scrumptiousness. "I'd have insisted on coming along before now."

"Enjoy it, dear heart, it's your one and only," Cat said.

"I don't know," Sydney said. "We don't entertain nearly as much as we used to, mixed company, I mean, do we Dan? I miss it. We should. This is fun."

"I think so too," said Dan. "You girls have had all the fun. Time to share."

"Are you thinking of one like this, or two, one with just us?" Maggie wasn't sure she wanted so much change. Too much had changed already.

"I'm not sure I can take Cat twice a year, but sure."

Joe glanced at Cat, assuming she'd take offense, but her reaching for another beer as though nothing had been said seemed to point otherwise. A grin from Dan told him this was normal. Joe just shook his head. He'd love to have more of these, if for no other reason than to watch his wife, whom he thought he knew so well, in action among her friends. How very much it took, how many years, to know someone. No wonder their loss of Cherry was so deep. He made up his mind to try even harder to help his beautifully complex wife through it.

"Hey, remember that time Cherry stripped down to her underwear and went for a swim?" complex Cat said to the girls, then turned to Jeff. "One too many brownies. Fun brownies."

A snug Sadie from her wrap in Sam's arms looked at Jenny with a wink, a reinforcing reminder her mother wasn't good at being under the influence. Jenny smiled, then gazed out at the water, along with everyone else, as if really watching a nearly exposed Cherry, as exposed as her life had become, romp in the waves. The spell held, silence fell, each thinking the same and watching as she invisibly faded into the water.

Then their Cherry was gone.

Does Rick return for Sadie? The Highland Six Pack's Sadie *answers that, it also resolves an unasked question from Book One, and brings the Pack into a surprising focus.*

R.S. Oatman

Made in the USA
Middletown, DE
23 November 2021

53254844R00091